Perfect Architect

Perfect Architect

Jayne
Joso

ALCEMI

First impression: 2011

© Jayne Joso, 2011

Published with the financial support of the Welsh Books Council

Editor: Gwen Davies
Cover design: Marc Jennings, www.theundercard.co.uk
Cover Images: Joerg Rainer Noennig
Internal Images: Hiroki Godengi

ISBN: 978-0-9560125-2-4

Printed on acid-free and partly-recycled paper.
Published by Alcemi and printed and bound in Wales by
Y Lolfa Cyf., Talybont, Ceredigion SY24 5HE
e-mail ylolfa@ylolfa.com
website www.alcemi.eu
tel 01970 832 304
fax 832 782

For Mum and Kiyoko Tamura and Setsuko Taguchi
&
in loving memory of
Nathalie Labbé

One of the basic human requirements is the need to dwell,
and one of the central human acts is the act of inhabiting,
of connecting ourselves, however temporarily,
with a place on this planet which belongs to us
and to which we belong.

Charles Moore, School of Architecture, UCLA
Foreword, *In Praise of Shadows*, Junichiro Tanizaki

In this world you have to be your hero.
By that I mean that you have to win
whatever it is that matters to you
by your own strength and in your own way.

Jeanette Winterson, *The Powerbook*

Chapter One
Perfect Architect

The Architect is dead.

He has choked on a piece of eel. Approximately 6cm by 8cm. She didn't even know he cared for eel. His wife, Gaia, is lost, and sorting through his things, for comfort, for legal matters and his clients, finds a bundle.

A bundle of letters.

Letter 1

Selené to Charles

My sweet Arles,

How wonderful are your ideas for the new house. All these long years of planning, of dreams, of secrecy, but soon we will all luxuriate in shared truth. At last! To be honest I think you star architects wait far too long before designing the 'dream home'. Why wait? You have had wealth and talent in abundance for donkey's years.

I can see the point in the workaday architects taking their time finding their feet, but that's hardly the case for those on the world stage, and not for 'name' architects such as you, Charles. Then again, a personality such as yours needs to prove itself, and only now when approaching the autumn of your life can you allow yourself your garden, your home, your true delight. As for me, well you know me more than any other, and I long skipped the hierarchies for mine own contentment. In fact, I think it not unfair to say that I have ignored them from the very start. You have always shown far more diligence than I.

Ah, fool. Men, you are all fools. I can sense that my teasing might make you mad, still, you must allow a girl her fun. I'd certainly never keep your attention if I did but only adore you, and adore you I do, Charles.

Again I congratulate you and await your next move.

My love to you as always

Selené

Letter 2

Selené to Charles

My dear Arles,

Oh sweet silly you. I see my last letter did inflame something in you. I mention the most lusty of seasons and you are made to feel old. Age so becomes a man. And Charles, you have far more to offer a woman now than ever before. You should rejoice! How proud you have become, but forgive me, it is a woman's want to inspire the flame of man from time to time. After all, someone has to check that one has not begun taking oneself *too* seriously.

As for women being the 'greater fools', I say not, for some of us have the good sense to keep you men at a wise and comfortable distance appropriate to our same requirements of say, the changes in season. And whilst you are in a brooding and disconsolate mood, pray take heed lest I decide to batten down the hatches in silence a while, I'm not good when a storm breaks.

My love to you as always

Selené

Letter 3

Selené to Charles

My sweet Arles,

Well in truth yes, perhaps a month's silence was too harsh, and for that I am sorry, but you have to admit that in overreacting I am not alone, and if I cannot remain free to speak as I wish, although my love for you would doubtless remain, I could no longer condone our relations further. I so love to tease, but that's always the way, and passions always peak in the wake of, and fear of losing them. Oh I am too cruel again. Forgive me, but the grass has been freshly cut, and I am of a mind to take a new lover. That luscious minted air arouses me more than the scent of any man, but then my affinity has always been with nature, and as you so often remind me, there are very few of humankind who I can abide or would abide me. I thought you might have left off the last part of that but I forgive you and assume it is but your possessiveness acting up.

Now then, that's enough for today my dear, I must just quickly sign off, do forgive me darling, but the little ones are acting up, and I myself am quite desperate for a change of scenery and some good fresh air. Heavens, I make such a poor mother. Anyway, I do hope you might visit us all soon, we miss you so.

My love to you as always

Selené

Gaia Ore, Swedish born, adopted by English parents; aged thirty-two, and alive. Charles Ore, half Norwegian, half English; and at the time of his death, forty-three, seven months, eleven days, four hours, and twelve seconds precisely. Detail was what Charles had lived, and indeed, died by. Had he no idea how difficult it was to choke on a piece of eel, how unlikely? And who counted the twelve seconds? Is choking so exactly measured? When dining with a fellow architect, it would appear to be the case. And Charles would have expected no less, though most others might have expected, and felt more appreciation of, a sharp pat on the back. Is architectural competition really so stiff? Apparently so.

Charles would have been supremely impressed by the statistics that upheld the most unusual, nay bizarre, of deaths. Though less impressed by the manner of it.

Gaia pored over the letters, some fifteen in the bundle, but coming back again and again to the most recent, the most personal, those she came to call: the final three.

The letters were in the same hand, from the same woman, all drenched in love and favour, and yes, intimacy. And what level of intimacy! To discover that this correspondence revealed that Charles, *Charles* had been given a pet name. Arles! A special, secret name, known to his secret correspondent, indeed perhaps to his *co-respondent*, and no doubt designed by the same. *Charles, Arles!* Gaia mocked. How trite, and unimaginative, simply cutting the first two letters. But how dare this... *this Selené*... have her own name for him? And who, pray... *is*... Selené? Oh yes, she is, *was* Charles' confidante, but what else? *What else?*

Secrets. Gaia and Charles had never had secrets.

She shivered, thinking, hoping, that perhaps the letters weren't his, that they belonged to another Charles, Arles! That they weren't there on the desk, that in fact, she had imagined them. Bereavement can do that to people, play tricks on them. It takes memories, real, and imagined, weaving them anew. Soiling them with pains, cleansing them with charity, with love, with fantasy. But it does not protect, bereavement is a feeble state.

A tear fell. A weighty tear, and it splashed dismissively onto the signature, smudging but not erasing...

...*Selené*

Sleep now for thought takes energies, and for now you are bereft.

Wasn't that his voice?

In his more gentle mood.

But sleep, sleep my sweet.

She let the letter fall next to its crumpled companions, and stole away to her study, to her sofa, a blanket, and deep exhausted sleep.

Chapter Two
The Construct

In the morning Gaia moved past the doorway of the bedroom, glancing in briefly to check that Charles wasn't there. And why would he, he had never been one for sleeping in. They had often slept apart. She trembled, remembering the call she had received just days before. A kind of guilt overcame her and she turned back and into the room. Gently she lay herself over Charles' side of the bed, running her hand over the pillow, wanting to weep. Unable.

She had to tell someone, had to find someone to tell. But most people knew already, and as he'd died whilst away on business, it was in fact *she* who was almost last to be told. And now of course it was in the press.

They had no family, few friends, and with his colleagues and peers she had always felt the need to retain a formal distance. But she must tell *someone*, must utter the news of his death in her own words, in her own voice, to prove that it was true. If she could just do that... somehow manage to say the words, see them acknowledged in someone else's face, his death in their expression, then it might just allow her to accept it as a reality. The desire felt brutal, but necessary.

She left the building in a state of disarray, clothes pasted on over pyjamas.

They lived in what Charles had insisted on calling the *Construct*, a concrete structure that comprised various *units*. One of the units was Gaia's study, and there she kept her own books to differentiate, he said, between her reading and his 'formal library'. In the study she also kept a television, which he couldn't bear, her plants, 'clutter', and her sofa-bed for the nights when Charles was sleep-working. The nights when his patience for the sleeper at his side would eventually cease, and he would ask that unless the marital partner was going to contribute in some way – by holding up vast sheets of paper in readiness for frantic sketching, or in supplying refreshment or necessary encouragement – she remove herself, that his room be limited to its useful elements.

Charles had proposed that they use the term 'home' only when it became entirely appropriate. That time being when he was satisfied with a design for such a place and when, in his estimation, their marriage had earned it.

Gaia moved from street to street, blind to her environment, to direction, to time. The streets were uniform, mapped out on a repetitive grid. In the far distance, and as yet unseen, was the man who delivered their mail, Tom Bradshaw. He was wearing his uniform, one that had seen few changes in its design over the years despite the numerous take-overs; Charles had commented as much. Tom and Charles had been on first name terms.

Gaia paused at a corner, realising that it must have been Tom who delivered Selené's letters – of course it was, and she sensed a bitterness erupting as though it made him complicit. But he was only doing his job and she liked him, though she hadn't known him as well as Charles had. You see, Charles was the early riser, the one up early enough to catch first delivery and pass the time of day over various packages, boxes and letters.

Tom had a wife, Cara, and two kids, Paul and Phoebe. Tom wanted "a whole stack of kids… that I can start a band with. I play guitar, guitar an'… we'd be called Poochi's Poops! How about that? Uh… Poo… Poo," but his nerves would get the better of his dreaming and his speech would dwindle to nervous silence. Charles would encourage him, he had a strange patience for the mailman that he didn't extend to many others. Charles kidded around with Gaia in the retelling, said it made him feel like he was back in the States, where real people's lives are like Updike's fiction. The Updike Documentaries, he called his episodes with Tom. Tom had spent his formative years in the States. Him and his wife Cara were childhood sweethearts.

Gaia had never really understood, she didn't read John Updike, she'd never lived in the US despite having wanted to. But like many dreams that she thought she and Charles had shared, their moving out to the States as a couple was something that never happened. Without realising and without intention, the number of 'shared dreams that never happened' had somehow multiplied, and after a time it seemed all the dreams were his. One personality subsumed by another; and just as Charles' passion, drive and talent exploded onto the world, Gaia's had gently fallen to one side. It was curious how easily this had happened, for Charles had certainly not intended it, not consciously at least. It had been a subtle erosion, an unseen tide lapping an open shoreline, with the sands of one dreamer slipping away and under. 'You've lost your verve!' Charles would say. And complicit somehow, she would laugh.

He suggested her verve might be spherical, a ball that had rolled away but might soon be found. They had even, when love still seemed to dust them lightly, looked for the ball under sofas and tables, scrambling about the floor on all fours like children. Then lain on their backs, like dying flies, but filled with warmth and still some laughter. Perhaps though, over time, the verve had rolled too far away. Perhaps it had been pushed. Either way, it was now very much harder to find. And Charles' capacity for fun had long been replaced by a sternness, a seriousness, a grown-oldness. Things had fallen apart, and somehow unseen, had not been mended.

Gaia thought back again to Charles' and Tom's Updike Documentaries. She held new suspicions about them. That these encounters were charged with the anticipation of further contact with a certain correspondent, a certain woman with whom a certain intimacy was shared. After all, to the over-educated upper-middle-class, heterosexual male, are mailmen really that compelling?

As well as children, Tom and Cara had a dog, a pit bull. Tom would joke with Charles about how it chased away any delivery people, especially their mailman, even biting him once. The dog bit other people too. Their neighbours wanted the dog dead, but Tom said it wouldn't be fair on the children, they loved Poochi, "Heck, they wanna name the band after him! Though I've always wanted to call us Pickles and Chillies."

Less than a year later, the dog mauled their newborn, Perry. Gaia had read about it in the local paper. Now the dog was dead too.

Unawares, Tom and Gaia traced the same pathway from opposite edges of town, he pausing to tease the mail through stiffened openings, she to look over her shoulder. Nothing and no one there. Just a dead field of streets. An easy concrete maze that would not permit the surrender to being lost. She wanted to walk somewhere less familiar.

Tom never read the papers himself, he preferred to hear the news straight from the streets, or through the windows of complaining women, over the breakfasts of frustrated men. He saw it as taking advantage of an essential editing service, "So... in... in... instead of me scouring the tabloids for what's up, and dredging through all the i-rrelevant, I just bide my time and let these good folk serve it up to me, piece by pretty piece."

And who could fault that for a method? That was the sort of tale that would tickle Charles, "I'd ask him how he coped when people's windows were not open!" Tom would smile, "Easy," he'd say, "I just knock the bastards up!"

So that was Tom, larger than life, heart enough for two.

His whistling could now just be made out. Losing her bearings, the buildings appeared to collapse one into another, the streets all repeats of the first one. The only difference between the ten connecting streets and the first was the Construct erected at one corner, the place that wasn't home.

Changing direction, Gaia moved from one street and sought comfort in back stepping down the connecting one. Startled, as she and Tom collided. He barely recognised her. No make-up, no perfected, frighted fashion on too thin bones. Today, she looked...? Well? Ordinary.

Gaia sensed his revised reading of her: she's no one really, when it comes down to it, under all that smartness, she's just like anybody else. To Tom that was nothing of an insult, for him, ordinary was as acceptable as anything else. But to Gaia it was wounding. She shot a look that pierced him through. Straight through his badge, uniform, T-shirt, flesh, bone. She remembered the letters, she looked at the bag on his shoulder, she wanted it, wanted the next letter, wanted to see what honest-Tom delivered to dishonest-dead-Charles.

16

"He's dead."

"Wha–z–s up…?" Had he heard that right?

"He's dead, Charles."

"Beg yo-ur pardon?"

"He's dead!"

Tom caught the widow awkwardly as her knees failed, but soon they were both to meet the pavement, and its cold cold slabs. The feel of the concrete sending shivers through them both. She pictured Charles laid out. She'd grazed the back of her hand to the knuckles, blood.

"I don't know wh… da…say…" Tom's words, falling away.

She looked into his face, he felt it and it panicked him, she might peel the very skin from his cheeks with such a cloying gaze. The blood drew back from his sharpening features, and a cold blue terror surfaced. And that was it. *That* was reflected death. Now it was real.

The concrete was disappearing, waxy, melting away. The mailman's haunted expression had unlocked the grief. The news burnt deep behind his skin and hurt. It hurt like hell.

A pale grey drizzle fell steadily.

He carried the widow to her place, took the keys from her pocket, removed the sodden outer garments, and delivered her to bed, the architect's bed. He had her drink some water, smoothed the curls out of her face, and promised to call back in a few hours. He wrote down a phone number and a message explaining that he had taken the keys so as to let himself back in, should she forget what had been said, and then he left.

She woke to the smell of fresh coffee moving through the various units and then the sound of Tom's voice from the floor below, "I don't know if you can hear me, I was ju–st saying, I'm not so used to the fresh stuff, but I think I'm getting to grips with the mech-anics of it." His voice was nearing, "Shall I, should I… well I was gonna suggest some music?" He reached the doorway, "But on second thoughts, that's… probably *in-*… appropriate… just got such a gigantic music system in this place. I've never been around inside before. Of course, I…."

Gaia smiled, Tom seemed so childlike and yet, she assumed, he must be about her age. Somehow the news of Charles' death, the letters, and telling Tom, all took the shape of strange fictional details and having wept so deeply she now felt deplete of emotion, any at all. No pain, love, nor worry, just a peculiar state of equanimity. She didn't want to analyse it. No emotion, and somehow that just seemed to fit.

Tom stood, his cheeks pink, feeling something akin to the awkwardness of a boy on the first day of something a bit too unfamiliar. Noticing; and then without meaning to, Gaia laughed.

"What's funny? Are you alright Mrs Ore?" She sat up, sensing the distance made by his formality. She wanted him to call her Gaia, but she didn't say.

"That tray must be heavy," she pointed to a table, "I'm sorry I laughed, I don't know why..."

"It doesn't matter, I don't think it's easy for you right now." He sucked up a breath, "I can't stay... I..."

Gaia sensed his feeling ill at ease, "No, no, of course... of course, but thank you..."

"Oh it's nothing. I just felt, sort of... well, duty bound, to check you was alright that's... all, and you're alright?"

"Yes, yes, and thank you... for being so kind."

He blushed again and withdrew from the room. Then as he left the house he called out again, he'd leave the keys near the mail on the table by the main door. The door slammed cleanly.

Mail, new mail.

Gaia bolted down the stairs, took up the envelopes almost without seeing them, and returned to the room. She let them fall onto the bed, then turned her back on them. Sudden resistance. Fear perhaps.

She breathed deeply, her eyes settling on a blanket, she pulled it around her shoulders and decided to try Tom's coffee first, now almost stubbornly ignoring the letters as they lay. – It made no sense. – But the contents of a letter, though very rarely, can sometimes cut too deep. She exhaled. Yes, a necessary delay.

Pouring the coffee, she began to look about the room. This, Charles' bedroom, was also called *creative-unit-four*, he numbered the rooms he worked in, there were seven in all. He had three actual workrooms, units, but somehow the entire building had given over its other functions to make still more space for their creative inhabitant. Kitchen, bathroom and so on, became almost redundant terms. The trouble was that cooking and bathing still had to happen despite the models, sketches, mappings, screens, and yet more models.

Behind a huge stretched-out roll of drafting paper, Gaia found a stack of heavy boxes. Dusty boxes. Dust wasn't especially unusual, Charles refused to have some areas of the units disturbed at all, and cleaning, by himself or anyone else, he found intensely disturbing.

She pulled one box out and blew at the dust. Lifted the lid. Letters. A full box-set of Selené. Pain shot up in her chest. She dropped the lid, went back to her own room and picked up her cigarettes.

Nicotine imbibed, she returned and began to tug at two other boxes, and damn her! There she was, entombed, enshrined, cut up and shared between three boxes, but not dead. And who knows, there might be more. She lashed the paper out of the way, kicked at model boxes, but no, there didn't appear to be any more. Selené – you fit into three boxes. You fit inside three boxes, and you fit into Charles' life, but how much of it? All of it? Have you always known him, known him longer than I have, better than I have?

She pulled at the letters, but was too distressed to open them, and in no mind to deal with the contents. Overwhelmed by the sheer amount, by what that meant, or *had* meant, or might mean, she pushed the letters back beside their dusty companions.

The cigarettes kept her hands busy, the coffee now made her shake. What to do? – Defeated, what greater harm could new mail do? – She went back to the bed and finally opened up the letters. Just bills. She clutched them to her chest. Strange to feel comforted by letters from the bank, the gas and electric supplier. She held on to them as she moved to look up and around this his favourite room, wondering now, just who had been the man that she had married?

Charles Ore had passed away without having achieved his 'home', and long before his potential could be realised, as architect, as intellectual, as man. He had fulfilled the dreams of many men's lifetimes by the age of forty, but Charles' potency had been that of his list of 'the great men of history' – of *Cusanus, Gropius, Rabindranath Tagore, Shostakovich,*

Lenin, Tom Waits… and Philip Roth, as he would say, *to name but a few,* and now it was cut short.

There was no corresponding list of great women, and Selené had suggested with great pride that these might simply have been too many to list. The real truth lay in Charles' belief that greatness, in all its philosophical dimensions at least, was limited to and encapsulated in the one consistent and overriding influence in his life, and that of course, was her, his dear beloved Selené.

Gaia now rose early to check the mail, but still nothing came from Selené. She quickly realised that Selené might actually be waiting for Charles' reply… to the last of the three. For would she know that Charles had passed away?

The sympathy cards piled up, arriving now from all over the world, from colleagues, rivals, friends from way back, from people Gaia did and did not know. A few even from admirers of Charles' work, fans you could say. Gaia thought it strange, but so it was with some of the more avant-garde architects, they were regarded for their brilliance in a way that seldom happened anymore, and certainly not outside the world of the architectural elite. Charles, ever cynical, would comment gruffly, "It seems we live in the shallows, and the present is too much given over only to celebrating the superficial… how people look… what they wear, dumb-ass branding and marketing… all the trash of modern life in place of talent, intellect and real hard work!"

Gaia felt a moment of pride in the cards and letters from his fans, perhaps Charles had re-elevated the status of the architect. *Re-elevation,* she smiled, the architect would have liked that. She moved through memories of times when she had caught his attention, when he had been interested or amused by things she had said. He hadn't always been only irritated by her. She wiped away an affectionate tear and smiled at one of his photographs, a more natural shot taken by a photographer from a broadsheet, she tried to recall which one. There had been many, and most were posed, half-shadow shots that somehow only ever revealed one persona, and it was not her favourite. Not Charles.

Chapter Three
The Widow's Letter

In the coming weeks a body was shipped, funeral arranged, attended, and Charles, buried. In the days that followed that, pangs of guilt as Gaia's thoughts about Selené shifted in emphasis. Perhaps she should have contacted her. Written to her. After all, Selené might not have known Charles was married, she might have been lied to, or at least kept in the dark about his wife's existence, as she had Selené's. Sympathy, but it was only momentary.

Charles had possibly lived a double life, but lies or none, it was Gaia that had been left to make all the arrangements, organise things, sort out legal matters, have his office advised as to how things were to continue in compliance with the will. And yet, if Selené had been duped, that made her an innocent, and though her right to grief was something Gaia questioned, she would undoubtedly feel some, whatever the rights and wrongs. She may even feel as much as Gaia, perhaps more.

What had she done?

She should have let Selené know. She should have invited her to the funeral. But that would have been too much to bear, still, she should have let her know.

She wandered through the units, picking things up, careful as she had always been, to put them back where she found them for fear of being scolded like a small inquisitive child – forgetting, in that moment, that he was dead.

Since finding the boxes, she had not returned to them, withered by the mere knowledge of their existence, the sheer amount, and fearful of the contents. Besides, the three most recent letters seemed to say it all, all and nothing, for they posed so many questions, and the various plausible answers seemed to multiply out of control, without reason to discipline them, without care of what they touched or how.

One thing remained clear, if Selené did not yet know of Charles' death, then she ought to be told. – Surely she would have read it in the papers by now. But even so, she ought to learn the news formally. Gaia would send a letter. It was only right. – Perhaps Selené knew someone in Charles' life… and they would have told her, certainly. But that couldn't be the case. Charles, whatever he had done, would not have risked compromising his work with the type of scandal and gossip which that would have generated. – Gaia settled to the belief that Selené was a well-kept secret, and that Charles would not have permitted her into other areas of his life. – She could barely believe her own thoughts, *how naïve!* The letters clearly indicated that Selené had access to Charles' most intimate thought processes at times – so who was she kidding? – *that Charles wouldn't let Selené in…* oh, she was in alright. *Right in!*

Cigarettes. She would have to go out and get more.

Inhaling, calming. No, Selené might know an awful lot about Charles, but she hadn't met with his team, with their few friends, it wasn't possible. Half a pack later, and Gaia realised that the inevitable had to be done, she would have to make contact, she would have to write that letter.

She wrote her own address, and then looked hard at Selené's, a PO Box address, why so? Why was part of her address a secret? Secrets, Gaia paused, then breathed deeply. Hadn't there been secrets enough already?

In order that she keep to the bare facts, to merely informing, Gaia put 'the final three' in the bottom drawer of the dresser in her room, that she would not continue rereading, reinterpreting, guessing at the implications of the contents. If she was to learn anything more about Selené, it would now have to be directly, with the woman herself, and not mediated through this loving correspondence with her husband.

She was aware that her desire not to write anything of a bitter letter was not at all the act of a tender heart. She simply had to ensure that Selené reply. She knew that if she wrote in any other language than that of formality, and possibly touching on compassion, the woman would never respond. And if she did not respond, then she would never get the kind of answers she was looking for. This letter was an opportunity to open things up, direct contact that might ultimately lead to direct answers, and she had to get it right.

After several false starts, frustrations over clichés, crying fits, and the last cigarette, Gaia finally composed herself well enough to write the letter to Selené that she would actually send.

Letter: To the Other Woman

Gaia to Selené

Dear Selené,

Forgive me, I do not know your name in full, indeed I do not know you at all, save for a few letters I have come across addressed to Charles Ore.

It is with deep regret that I inform you of his death, the nature of which I would rather not go into, except to say that he did not suffer terribly, nor for long. I'm afraid I must apologise further, the funeral has already taken place, and Charles laid to rest. I think that this news must come as a terrible shock to you, and with these few words I send compassionate and sincere wishes.

In sympathy

Yours

Gaia Ore

Gaia immediately sealed the envelope, addressed it and set out to send it right away. She grabbed a long coat, pulling it over her pyjamas as she dashed out of the door, in her haste failing to notice her footwear, just socks and old slippers. *His* old slippers, and several sizes too big. Gaia had never worn slippers, preferring thick socks that were the intended partners of hiking boots. The socks at least helped fill out some of the excess space, but still, she was likely to trip.

The paving and Gaia were becoming too familiar, and in so short a space of time it was something of a whirlwind affair, so often forced cheek to cheek. She blushed. This time grazing her face, as the fall was greater, and with no mailman to break it with a gentleman's excuse me. Who designed these stupid slabs? Not Charles, she sniffed to herself. Her spine had twisted a little, some muscles pulled. Slight twinges of pain would later remind her of this second close brush with the ground.

In the post office, people in the queue noticed the slippers. Some kids laughed at her. She felt herself colour again.

She looked about, connecting the mail in her hand with Tom; and the fall to the one she had experienced with him all those weeks before. He wasn't there. Of course not. She bit into her bottom lip. With all the tension and embarrassment, she had partly crushed the envelope, she flattened it back out as best she could, but it still looked rather crumpled. It was too late to change it, to go back to the Construct and rewrite it afresh. If it was to be sent at all, it had to be done now, had to be over with. Her mouth was too dry for the stamps, she asked for the self-adhesive kind.

"They're all self-adhesive now, have been for ages," said the girl at the counter without looking up.

Quiet tears tumbled down Gaia's face, stinging the cut cheek as they moved.

Stamps attached, she pushed the letter toward the girl.

"No. Box is outside," said the girl, "you put it in yourself."

Despite feeling pinched, Gaia was glad at least that their eyes had not met. She shuffled now over the intense stripy carpet to the world outside, found the box, bid the letter goodbye. It was done.

Now all she had to do was wait.

Chapter Four
The Waiting

In the days dividing sending and receiving, Gaia barely ate, washed nor breathed. She soon gave up trying to distract herself. For what could possibly take her attention away from the gathering strength of Charles and Selené's relationship? Oh yes, Charles was dead, but for Gaia, the illicit relationship was alive, kicking, and thriving. It increased in her mind with each new breath. The more she thought, the more she imagined, the more magnified the relationship and all the possibilities. It became, however unwittingly, a self-torture.

Empty cigarette packs now littered her study and his room, *creative-unit-four*, the room where she presumed he had written his side of the correspondence. Bitterly she thought, his *creative-fornication-unit*.

Language, Charles would play around with it ceaselessly, "Gaia," he would say, "it is the most natural preoccupation of artists to play with language, *especially architects*. Pushing its usage to its limits and far beyond; mixing the sounds of words in one language with their meaning and use in another, and also creating entirely new terms." There were times, however, when Gaia felt aggravated by Charles' contributions to the linguistic mix.

"Gaia, sweet Gaia, language simply doesn't interface well enough with architecture. Architecture moves, morphs even, *much much faster* and with protean leaps! Language makes a poor attempt to keep pace, and with the English language, there are simply too many words, yet never the ones to explain well enough!" Besides Norwegian, he was competent if not entirely fluent, in English, German, Russian and, as Selené had oftentimes remarked, "As much as you claim to abhor the same, dearest Charles, you are quite the native when it comes to *Public-Relations-Speak*." Gaia was often made overly aware of his egocentrism, and that, she recalled, was a word he mistakenly thought she had created herself, "Ah, ego-centr-ism! Well done, sweet Gaia. You see, *finally* you begin to learn the art of language tricks through me!"

Like many other things, Gaia now wanted to discuss this ego, this boundless ego, with Selené.

She took out the final three, scouring them afresh for new instruments of torment. For that was all they could offer. Clear answers could only come from the woman herself, but the waiting was hard. It was strange, but each time she looked at the letters, she seemed to read something new. The words had been there all the time, but perhaps a mind in a state of distress edits out some parts, that the reader is exposed to only a number of upsetting aspects and not an immeasurable torrent.

Gaia's attention settled on Letter 3, and the mention of 'little ones', of Selené being 'a poor mother' and how they 'missed' Charles 'so'. Tears slipped. But Gaia was sure this couldn't mean Charles' offspring. Surely. He had always been vehemently against having children. Gaia had thought to persuade him. Time had run out. No, she was fairly sure this couldn't be the case, and Charles was not the sort of man to have been easily trapped into such a situation. Gaia ran her own words back in her mind. How did she know *what sort of man Charles was*, or had been? Perhaps he loved Selené in a different way, in a way that had influenced him enough to have a child, children even. Perhaps this *Selené* had tried to trap Charles by becoming pregnant. Certain women do indeed make quite cunning 'trapists', Gaia felt pleased – a genuinely new term, *that* would have raised a smile in Charles. Cunning trapist, cunning-trapist, *cunt!* Tears erupted. She tore the letter down its centre and imagined it as the woman herself, cutting through her very centre – mind, womb, sex. Had this woman stolen a right that was hers? Gaia's hands shook. She wanted to reign in these gruesome thoughts.

Halfway through a cigarette, Gaia picked up the two parts of the letter, ashamed at her violent thoughts, alarmed by her own language. She rarely swore, and when she did, her vocabulary was limited. How incredible are the barriers that extreme emotions tear through. Somehow there were no limits. Not anymore.

She realised that until now she had worked on the assumption that the relationship was entirely down to Charles, that he must have taken the role of predatory, pursuant male, when on the contrary it might

27

have been in the grips of the female. Selené, what woman are you?

She sobbed and beat the pillows of the sofa-bed. She knew that dramatic explanations pushed away the more plausible, more painful scenarios, but simply couldn't bear to think of their being in *love* in some substantial tender way. And all this emotion was taking her strength by stealth. Such erosion leading to greater and greater slips, she might soon face a more complete collapse.

The end of the pack. Ripping the cord of another, but the tension in her chest forced her to release her grip. The fresh cigarettes tumbled to the floor, and she slept.

The reply would come soon enough.

A Spanish Architect...

In Northern Spain, Carlos Santillana wanders about the local market, reflecting on the design meeting from that morning, and unaware that he will soon be one of a select group of architects invited to compete in designing a home for The Architect's Widow. A home for Gaia Ore.

Carlos describes his work as *sensual architecture*, "Buildings that connect with the same number of senses any good person might possess, and *more!*" He laughs mildly to himself, thinking back on the fool engineers he has been in meetings with, at how senseless, how impotent they seem. He thinks, in fact, that all people have at their disposal far more senses than they ever care to mobilise. Engineers! *Argh!* How could you expect sensitivity! He laughs again, and finds himself under the perusal of a small girl at the hem of her mother's titanic skirt. Big eyes. He laughs some more in response and smiles in her direction, she quickly smiles back, then embarrassed, coils herself in the flow of skirt, and is entirely lost save for two stick legs and tiny feet in her new textile habitat.

Following his death, Charles Ore assumed a level of acclaim that far outshone his idolisation in life. Perhaps that now made him a saint among architects, though doubtlessly he'd have favoured such adoration to acknowledge him for having a devilish more than saintly nature, and that would have been far closer to the truth. Charles became known as *The Architect of the Age*, an achievement that is sadly only ever offered posthumously. And as competitors, the dead always prove the most difficult to defeat. Carlos, however, always took life's trials in his stride, and to him, an epitaph was simply that, it held little currency as far as he was concerned, in the living world. The two men had had little in common, but their drive and passion for architecture had run almost parallel, and whilst Charles lived, they had been contenders.

Carlos drew his inspiration from nature and from his studies of nomadic tribes; and he talked about his profession, as he did his children, with the deepest and most profound love. "You know what's great about architecture?" and like the world's best storytellers he would wrap you gently in words and warmth, "Well... let me tell you. It's that you start with nothing, from nowhere; a ground with nothing on it, empty, and you draw something, something that's going to come out from the earth. You can take anything, anything at all, the most basic materials, sticks, rocks, anything you like... cow dung if you choose!" His big eyes glistened, "Dung, nice... it can make very good rendering... adequate at least... from horses, from cows, whatever's nearby!" His hands now moulding the air, sketching in space, "You can even make bricks from this shit if you like! You would have to compress them... coat them in something, conditions must be right... no rain, but the point is that you must not feel limited!" And then slowing up smoothly to regroup his thoughts, "But the excitement, the *real excitement* about architecture comes from seeing this nothingness change... an empty space transformed, maybe a habitat emerging there, a little oriental tearoom, a school, a hospital, a gallery... *something comes where once it was not.*" He rubbed his ample belly in gentle satisfaction, "*That is what's great about architecture.*"

Carlos' current preoccupation, nay obsession, with transient architecture would regularly send him into a state of complete delirium. His wife, Fabiola, would try to restrain more than calm him. Her device, heavy cooking, nutritious no doubt, but with the accent firmly on cementing her husband to the spot for a period of more than thirty minutes, lest he run wild again with ranting, and wake the children! They had five, and more would surely come; natural rhythms they did indeed triumphantly embrace, yea, endorse! Trumpets yielding, bugles hollering, a regular sexual fanfare. Charles, on the other hand, had always felt that a degree of sexual tension was a necessary spur to the creative spirit, and that to merely *give in* to it in so obvious a way was to render oneself slave to one's 'sexual self'. Carlos was given to the view that the natural release of sexual energies would lead to the promotion of entirely new and intensely invigorating ones, at least as rich and strong as their seed. Charles would never have accepted such a theory, advocating restraint to the point of abstinence, and celebrating with great pride his own capacity for discipline in this area. His energies would not be so diffused. For Carlos such a mindset was far too serious, too far from what nature intended, too much at odds with the balance of life.

Charles had been irked by his Spanish counterpart, and this was made evident, as always, in his choice and misuse of words, "No, over-indulgence in the sex act, it don't lead that way, no, not to the *promotion of new energies*, it leads only to the production of babies!" And this with the flavour of his abhorrence of reproduction in general, and overpopulation in particular.

In conversation with the mailman, Charles had been much softer and more tolerant of the idea of the large family. But Tom had a quality that touched Charles in a way that almost no one else could. And the fact that Tom's procreation had some real purpose behind it, namely creating the band members for Poochi's Poops, was close enough to justifiable reason in Charles' mind. Making people for no reason, the result of mere contraceptive negligence, well that was no good reason at all. Making a band, well, there was a place for that, if people will have children. – Charles voiced his opinions fervently until he finally realised his minority view largely fell on deaf ears.

During his university days, women were infuriated by him, arguing that all mothers and would-be-mothers should be given help and support by society. Charles agreed, "Yes, certainly they should. Society should tie their tubes at twelve! And they should remain that way until they can prove themselves and the fathers, capable of good parenting; until they can offer good reason for adding to an already overpopulated world, and until they can financially and emotionally support both themselves and their offspring!" Eventually, he would grow tired, "There's no point in talking with fools, people will do what they will, and I… I will do… what I will!"

The discussion of population growth and its social and architectural implications was one that architects came back to time and again, particularly those who designed for cities. Charles and Carlos had not often crossed paths but when they had, Charles would berate the Spaniard, "In the coming twenty-five years, the population will explode by half its number again! Fifty per cent increase, doesn't that frighten you?" But fear could not penetrate this most positive of souls, and Carlos would never envisage new lives as anything less than the world's rich bounty. "Just think how much more love there will be in the world, Charles, with all those new hearts beating."

31

Charles would have easily committed Carlos Santillana to memory in the pejorative sense, were it not for the fact, that despite talking almost nothing but utter drivel, the man stood on the point of the architectural horizon that glows brightest. Santillana was one of a generation of maestro designers and creators, and not even Charles could deny it.

Chapter Five
The Reply

Selené to Gaia

Dear Mrs Ore,

I should like to call you Gaia, but make no such presumption, though I very much feel I know you, and sense a closeness to you without ever having met. No, I must remain formal. I sense my knowledge of you might be greater than yours of me, and so you are at a disadvantage. I hope this will not always be the case. My dear girl, how horribly unhappy you must be. I share in your grief, but naturally, as his wife, you must be in such awful pain, oh dear me, would that I could come there and comfort you. However, I am perhaps the most afflicted misanthrope, and suffer various other indulgent phobias, probably mostly imagined, as Charles would say, but nonetheless I really cannot for the life of me leave my home, much as I should like to. Please accept my great affection towards you, oh dear girl.

Once you feel able, I hope that you might write to me again. I think there are things you may be desirous of knowing; Charles, he was a secretive soul.

My deepest sympathies

Selené

Gaia felt the disadvantaged position Selené spoke of, and *how* she felt it. She had achieved the initial goal of having Selené reply, but the letter betrayed almost no new information. What it did succeed in was feeding an already distraught soul, and affirming certain suspicions.

I hope that you might write to me again. I think there are things you may be desirous of knowing.

How dare this woman be so bold as to *invite* the widow's questions, weren't these hers by right, and not at the co-respondent's leisure? And what shameless vanity, that Selené seemed so willing to parade her relationship with Charles. Enough of this! Gaia knew what she wanted. Clarity. Direct answers to direct questions.

She looked over the letter again, examining it closely, she felt it mocked her; and now she also deeply resented the degree of familiarity in which it was written, the assumed sense of closeness. It grated.

No more of this.

The gloves were off.

Things I'd be *'desirous of knowing'*, damn you! That's exactly right, *Selené!*

Gaia took up her pen.

After a determined start, Gaia's rage lost its impetus, and the letter was to become a simple one. In truth, all the aggressive, angry emotions were something of an anathema to her, and try as she might, they were not robes cut to her more tolerant, tranquil shape.

Her thoughts soon directed her towards retaining a certain amount of civility, for the time being at least, lest she accuse the adulterous woman of further crimes without *sufficient evidence*. – And whatever her feelings, this correspondence had to be maintained, the letter had to be sent, and the faster she sent it the faster the reply would come.

Letter: To the Co-respondent

Gaia to Selené

Dear Selené,

Why do you address me as – *My dear girl*? I can't imagine why you should choose such language.

It appears that Charles was indeed secretive. Your relationship seems to have quite a history, perhaps it even predates his and mine? You suggest I might want to know more of your relationship. I do.

Bereaved as I am, finding out that another woman has shared your husband comes as perhaps an even greater shock than if he were still alive. But I do not want sympathy.

In one of your recent letters to Charles you spoke of 'little ones', will you enlighten me? I thought I had many more questions, but somehow that's sufficient for now.

Yours

Gaia Ore

Letter: To the Agitated

Selené to Gaia

Dear darling Gaia,

Dearie dearie me, your pain is almost palpable! It is to be expected of course. But how I wish I could be of some help.

You seem most distressed somehow by 'me'? Is it so very awful not to have been singular in Charles' affection? It comes as something of a shock to me, but perhaps it is due entirely to Charles having kept us secret. I have to confess, that was at my request. Something I made him commit to as a child, and he, as diligent and loyal a man as he grew to be, did not fail me in that, as he would no one. But then that must be obvious to you now. I'm sure such qualities are part of what must have drawn you to him.

Oh, and I am all but forgetting your questions, you see, I am of far less reliable character than Arles! Now then let me just pour myself a drink, I feel most drawn to tears again, quite sentimental, and after my drink I shall return to what you ask.

Now, where was I? Ah yes, my relationship clearly does predate, as you put it, yours and Charles'.

You mention the little ones, yes and now I must tend to their needs. I do hope this letter helps you some. Write again soon dear.

With love

Selené

Letter: In Anger

Gaia to Selené

Dear Selené,

You do lack Charles' diligence, yes! You have not answered my questions, not at all. You just pussyfoot around. Haven't you done enough? Is it your aim now to torment me?

When I said that your relationship was longer than mine, I wanted to know exactly *how long*? I thought that would have been obvious! Alright, you've known him since childhood, but have you been close all that time, were you childhood sweethearts before becoming adult... adult lovers?

And you evaded entirely my enquiry as regards the little ones! What game do you play?

Yours

Gaia Ore

Letter: To the Mislead

Selené to Gaia

Dear Gaia,

Firstly, let me offer my profuse apologies to you dear girl. What have I done!

Although I was kept secret from you, in my own silly way I somehow thought that you had now come to know me. Thoughtless of me really. And I suppose it is a kind of arrogance in my character that has assumed that I can actually put myself in my letters. I was at pains to work out your anger until your line about *childhood sweethearts* and *adult lovers*. Lovers! Goodness me, Arles and I? No! Darling Gaia, my sweet sweet girl, I am above seventy! So you see, some thirty years plus when he was but a child. That was in the days before I became so reclusive; I knew his parents quite well. I probably shouldn't say this, but a part of me is flattered that my hand and turn of phrase has not betrayed my age. I look back at your earlier letter and see that you did ask me something about the language I use, and that you couldn't quite fathom it. But I think that were you not already in a state of grief, your normal faculties would have cleanly traced that I belong so much less to your time, and so much more to an elder one. Sweet jealous Gaia. You know, Arles would have been so proud to have raised such intense emotion in you. He loved you so. I hope this knowledge allows you to relax in some measure. No my dear, I was never your husband's lover, I was merely an old, adoring, not-even-blood-related sort of aunt.

Now then, where was I up to with your questions? Ah yes, 'little ones', my King Charles spaniels, darling. I have six. Little tinkers! I hope, given the great misunderstanding, that you were not under the illusion that I had borne Charles any children. Heaven forbid! I can't really follow that if you did; he so proudly showed off the receipt for his vasectomy, I remember it very clearly. His parents were mortified, and that shortly before their deaths. Terrible. He was just twenty-six as far as I remember.

As for myself, I have taken many lovers over the years, and saw no need to take a husband. And not inclined towards children I have none of those either. I have very little inclination toward people at all, save from a distance.

I do hope I have covered everything this time. Oh you poor girl, do not despair. I also hope that our early correspondence will, in time, prove to be the subject of laughter in future years. Of course, you cannot see it now, but believe me, your life will on, it will on and on darling. I sense your weakness now, but you will not pass away with Charles, so help me, you will not.

My greatest affection

Selené

That the peculiar turn of phrase turned out to be that of an elderly aunt figure and not of a patronising seductress, was substantially humbling. Gaia collapsed into herself as the news intensified and fell upon her in monstrous embarrassment. The relief she should have felt, knowing she had not been betrayed to any great degree, if at all, was withered by the knowledge of her own gross foolishness and sheer misplaced spite.

She had designed Selené in full; flesh, disposition, age… yes – and what had she for material? Arguably almost nothing. She had designed her from the spaces between the lines in three brief letters. She had made far too much from far too little. But the boxes! Three boxes! But she hadn't examined the contents, and had she done, she may so easily have allayed all her own fears. She could have done so, and without having humiliated herself.

Whiskey and cigarettes.

And more cigarettes.

The last letter contained so much, she read it over, brushing the curls from her eyes and forehead, and tears that had fallen to her cheeks. Yes, there it was, *vasectomy* at *twenty-six*. Charles and Gaia had never had secrets, but Charles had. Yes, Charles had had secrets, and Charles and Selené had had secrets.

Gaia and Charles had married when she was twenty-five and he, thirty-six. He had openly declared from the outset that he did not want to have children. He had not declared however, that he had already taken action to make this de-cision, by means of in-cision, a *fait accompli!* Gaia was exhausted; emotions, so many, so varied, and so fast. Her chest felt constricted. She put out the cigarette in her hand. She drank some water. Lots of water. Whiskey, ultimately, wasn't going to help, certainly not make clear her thoughts. She slept for thirteen hours, drank more water, and slept thirteen more. Charles couldn't bear the idea of sleeping more than seven hours at a stretch, he'd thought it, unsurprisingly, a hideous waste of time.

Chapter Six

Critters

Whilst Carlos Santillana works out his sensual aspirations in Spain, English architect, Edwin Ray, wanders about his spacious London office. He's been drinking. Red wine. He looks across the room and eyes his black Scottish terrier.

Proudly named, The Scotsman, the dog is appropriately independent, self-assured, and perhaps most importantly, an astute judge of character. Edwin wonders what The Scotsman will make of their impending visitor. A journalist. A very young journalist from a large Sunday paper according to his assistant's most recent note. – Gathered over a number of years, the assistant's notes now run to a colossal number, and piled up high, form a series of elegant spiral towers on Edwin's desk. A fragile, high-rise, city of paper.

As he waits for the journalist to arrive, Edwin begins to wonder, somewhat anxiously, what he might be asked. He genuinely doesn't care for interviews, certainly not outside the academic arena – perhaps he should have asked to see the questions in advance... and will the youngster notice things, things that really matter? *Things that speak?*

He glances at the dog, then along his long, elegant desk, designed, like everything else in the office, by himself. He smiles and takes another sip of wine.

Twenty years earlier, someone rather special had noticed. Someone *very special indeed*, he corrects the thought. Lizzie. And she, not an architect herself, not at all, though he speculated that under different circumstances she might have been. Lizzie was a singer; played the violin too. Edwin glanced back towards the door, a momentary warmth of feeling, but she wasn't there. More's the pity.

Twenty years earlier, Lizzie had been his girlfriend. She had visited Edwin in his very first apartment, the first he had owned, and very quickly she began to notice things, and in detail too. Lizzie looked at things and saw them in a way that most people did not – it amazed

Edwin just how few people observed their surroundings at all well. "So many people look, but precious few *see.*" – And this he thought of as chief among reasons for bad design. Designers and architects who do not see, design badly – and any population encountering this simply has to live with it! Like it or lump it. Shameful. – But Lizzie, oh she clearly had an eye.

He indulged his thoughts a moment longer, shooting back to Lizzie's observations of his very first home. Of course, the paper chairs were easy, clearly home-made affairs. Cardboard packaging, layer upon layer, strength enough to take the weight of a full-grown man. She had been amazed. He had glowed. Yes, amazed was she, and quite soon dazzled. Was it right for a man to be quite so tremendously adored? – He wanted Lizzie to be free to wander about the place by herself, to make her own discoveries and so, for the time being, he'd limited himself to the kitchen space. He would cook them dinner. In those days he did that, seemed to enjoy it too. – Distantly he heard Lizzie move about the place, a door open, a cupboard door slide to one side. He listened keenly, and guessed to himself what it might be that she was looking at.

She called out about the bed, had he made that? Yes. He'd felt himself blush. – He might make a sauce, if he could remember the recipe well enough. Mustn't let it boil, he knew that much. It was all in the fine tuning, so to speak. Use a wooden spoon, *no no*, the spatula. Stir, but only gently. Certain things take time.

He could hear her gentle tread, she was back in the living room. She tapped her fingers along the glass and steel dining table. Did she like it? Might it be too industrial looking for her taste? Did singers like such metals and glass in close proximity? Might they prefer a world of wood? Something more earthy perhaps, seemingly natural?

Some of the furniture was from his student days, very finely finished though. And even some of the early pieces had known exhibition space. The oil drum chair had caused great amusement. Quite an act in balancing to secure the buttocks on such a precarious thing, but nonetheless, once sat, most accepted it was a rather marvellous thing.

But would Lizzie understand the need to experiment, would she be capable of seeing it as something more than some mad eclecticism, a recycling frenzy of materials? For what better way to understand materials than to have the greatest fun with them? He stirred the pot with vigour, his shyness, his need to impress making him ridiculous now. The sauce would get the better of him today. No matter. And perhaps it wasn't always good to introduce sauce into a relationship too soon. He wasn't sure.

"All of it?" She was standing in the doorframe.

Edwin jumped. "Pardon me?" though there was nothing whatever the matter with his hearing.

She ran her fingers along the kitchen cupboards, tapping, blue, red, yellow.

"You made it, didn't you? Everything. Every last stick of furniture here. You made it all." She stood, shoulders wide and proud.

"That's right," he responded. Part of their dinner now starting to catch on the bottom of a pan. Can't be good at everything, thought Edwin. He moved the pan from the flame and smiled. No, no need for sauce.

Would he tell this tale to the journalist? Perhaps not. Too private. Besides, the romance had not ended well and most probably a reporter would not settle until he'd heard it all, and dredged up the more painful aspects of the relationship. He should have treasured Lizzie, he knew that now. The Lizzies of the world don't pass your way that often. He was too young back then, too ambitious. And Lizzie eventually had fled; had a child with someone else; and now made albums, a worldwide success.

It had been a case, he decided, of bad timing. Broken hearts. His at least. No, this wasn't for general consumption, despite the delightful opening.

But then, what would he be prepared to discuss? What indeed? For he knew how tricky interviews could be, easily too personal; and journalists... how they attempt to lead you astray... but more than anything he did not want to be drawn on things which did not interest him. He resolved that he would not be.

He put his hand to his chin and wondered now if he should have trimmed his beard. No matter. It was only the press.

He topped up his wine.

Germany! Why didn't he think of it before? This must most certainly be included.

Before opening his office in London, Edwin had spent a good many years in Germany, and he often thoroughly regretted his return to England. Ah, *Germany!* Inwardly he would sigh. A mix of nostalgia, admiration and deep lament. Germany, where architecture was still a truly intellectually rigorous discipline, where project managers were treated with appropriate disdain, if indeed they were appointed at all; a place where at least his thoughts could run free, though the number of realised projects, he had to admit, was rather less than he might have hoped for. No matter. – But in Germany, architecture was still held as a very serious intellectual pursuit, and that he deeply mourned, "Only in Germany, only in Germany... well... and the United States," he would concede, though he cared rather less for the latter. Yes, he would endeavour to communicate something of these feelings in the interview.

An assistant emerged from an adjacent room. The journalist had arrived. Should he show him through? The architect nodded. The Scotsman wagged his tail.

The young journalist had naturally expected and accepted that a member of Edwin's staff would set the meeting up, he knew that direct access was out of the question, especially given Edwin's status – but later, when he learned that Edwin Ray had never used email in his life and that he refused even to touch a phone, he had all but squealed in disbelief – delight almost, at what he would later write up as firm evidence of the architect's eccentricity. Of course, *cell* and *mobile* had their meanings, but in Edwin Ray's mind these were not closely related to conversation. And if the young journalist was interested to note down further trivial detail, neither did the architect drive, he had never learned. "Busy, you see. But I *can* draw, and some say I can build!" He chuckled warmly.

The journalist remained in half shadow. In awe. The Scotsman padded about the office space in keen anticipation.

Edwin couldn't make sense of the young man. Hovering there in the shadows... come into the room properly, it's not a Hitchcock movie!

But Ernest Wrightsin, double-first-from-Oxford aside, socialised by the bold and the brash, was quite simply, nervous as hell. The Scotsman sniffed around the cuffs of the man's trouser legs. Unlike his owner, The Scotsman rather enjoyed company, but he remained dutifully aware of Edwin's rather more misanthropic nature. What to do?

"*Well?* Are you coming in or is that simply your very favourite spot?" The architect now terrorised the acoustics with a baleful belly-gripped whoop. The journalist, struck at the ears, now shook his head in an attempt to release the pressure and moved forward gingerly.

The Scotsman grew concerned. This encounter might require a particularly watchful eye. For the time being he returned to his blanket and box, strategically positioned halfway up the staircase, his observation tower.

"I'm most grateful to you, Mr Ray…"

"Haven't told me your name?"

"My name?"

"Yes," answered Edwin curtly, "I know my own."

"Oh… it's Wrightsin, Ernest. That is, Ernest Wrightsin. Wrightsin Ernest."

Edwin chuckled, Ernest blushed.

"Anyway," the architect continued, summoning the man deeper into the space, and directing him to take a seat upon his award winning, Leipzig Lounger, "you come on in now, right in. That's right. Now sit."

The journalist, immediately emasculated, obediently sat; he could feel the blood draining from his cheeks and finger tips. He'd seen the Leipzig Lounger in magazines, he'd seen them in exhibitions, and now… now he was sitting upon one, the architect-designer himself standing before him. It was all he could do to breathe. Should he say as much? Too gauche?

He noticed the spiral paper towers on the desk, he hoped he would remember to ask about them. He wanted, more than anything, to ask intelligent questions. He wished he'd written them down.

Sensing that the atmosphere between the two men was still quite uncomfortable, The Scotsman tootled back over and wagged his tail some. Humans, he had noted, were apt to misjudge things, and a little

45

more sensitivity was sometimes required. He glanced up at Edwin in an attempt to convey as much.

For a few awkward moments the architect now paced a perfect concrete floor. The light gently altering the lines, shadows marking out the space. A silence emerged and it lasted a little too long.

"Sexy, isn't it?" said Edwin suddenly.

"What?"

"The floor, damn you."

"Sexy?... Er, that's not the first adjective that springs to mind...."

Edwin looked the young man over, maybe he wasn't as dumb as he looked, and *sexy* had merely been a test. – As one of the world's greatest architectural intellects, and as a stout and proudly heavy-set man, Edwin knew how intimidating the press could find him, specially the young skinny ones. The boys who'd never been made to build even a damn wall in their lives; never had a thought they could call their own. *Ninnies*, he would say.

"And so, what adjective would you offer my floor then?"

"I wouldn't give it any... not at first. Look... I... I'm rather more interested in discussing space, new topographies... and, well something I'm particularly interested to know, is... *is how come... how come you've resisted the new freedoms opening up to architects?"* Ernest gasped for breath.

Edwin raised an eyebrow. Now *this*... just might prove to be interesting. It might also call for more wine. "Go on," said Edwin.

Sensing the architect's favourable change in tone, The Scotsman retreated to his cardboard bed and blanket. Things might just settle down. Besides, there was a treat hidden in that blanket.

The journalist braced himself, and now, pushing up through his guts full pelt he declared, and rather bravely, "Well... well it just seems to me, that despite pushing architecture intellectually, both in your published works, and in your theoretical works, you seem determined almost... resistant almost, to putting it into practice, you know... in *actual... realised...* building projects."

"I do?" Edwin's ears now pricked up, The Scotsman's also. "Perhaps so," mused Edwin, now fully engaged. "But you must be wary of several things here," he paced a little more, "that architects are not simply designers who sup on red wine, though partial to it…" Edwin had amused himself with these last words and his eyes sparkled. His mouth watered and he looked back across the desk to the distant bottle, tantalising. But no, in a moment, for now he had this young-thing in his midst, and so he continued, "…that you do not place realised architectural projects over and above the theoretical – *But real architecture is more important! Buildings are built to last! Buildings are monuments!* – I see it in your eyes. But right now, and by way of example, the Spanish architect, Santillana, specialises in the 'transient' possibilities of architecture," he mournfully drained the last in his glass and went on, "what that might imply for refugee populations, the homeless, the explosion of people who inhabit inner cities and also those suddenly converging on previously low populated rural areas, and more than that, in disaster areas; I don't want to digress too far, but you see my point. And let's face it, whilst Hitler had that Albert Speer fellow build him architecture to last a thousand years, ultimately it matters not how tough or how tall you build, nature or man can *fall-it-down* just as sure as you ever *put-it-up*. Think about it boy! Earthquakes! Terrorists! War! That said, an awful lot of Hitler's buildings remain intact. Heavens… um," he would have to refill that glass, and soon, "apart from that, a man of integrity," here he gritted his teeth, doubting any journalist's ability to appreciate this aspect, "a man of integrity cannot simply give in to the moods and sways of current fashions if they are not already part of his artistic inclination, nor part of his developing philosophy. Besides there is only so much ground for the rather flash type of project you're referring to, I think you have the Italian in mind, Cannizzaro?" The journalist was slightly cowed, coloured by his own predictability. He could not speak. No space for it. Edwin carried on, "Alessandro Cannizzaro, ah! And Italy!" He glanced again at the bottle, "I've always been of the same opinion as Charles Ore when it comes to Italy – terrible loss, that man – no, they have no real sense of urgency, of getting the project finished. I mean, in the UK one can find oneself somewhat stifled by dratted project management, and intellectually starved at times, but we do at least get the job done. The Italians however, well I suppose it's the heat. – The point is… that these *new freedoms* of which you speak, must not simply lead to *novelty architecture*, oh no, that's something that really must be guarded against."

"Right."

"Right? Do you mean by that… that you comprehend, you agree… or that you are merely embarrassed at your gaucheness?"

The Scotsman shot Ernest Wrightsin a look by way of instruction. Ernest appeared to comprehend. "All of the above!" he answered quickly.

Edwin laughed and several inches of midriff danced merrily in satisfaction. "I think you know I care little for you journo-critic types, *critters* I call you when you're out of earshot! Wine? Red wine?" He didn't wait for a reply but administered the drink as to one who was dying and would surely be glad of anything that might possibly save them.

"Critter you." He patted the young man on the back, almost shattering his fragile bones, the journalist felt himself quake. "Yes, never liked critics, press… whatever else you call yourselves. – The critic is a particularly negative position to take up. Just as the organs of the body divide into those with positive aspects such as the brain and heart, and those with negative concerns such as the liver or kidneys, which largely deal with breaking things down and with waste… *you boy, are the liver!*" he laughed on heartily, and then added, "Perhaps the critic will get a better deal in the next life, eh? And… perhaps not. And Lord knows I'm no ruddy Buddhist!" The *ist* of Buddhist whistled through wine-teeth. The journalist flinched, he was still pretty new to the game, but something told him – namely the tape running in his pocket – that he'd just got himself a plum interview, and what would he call it?

That Critter – The Architect, Edwin Ray, in Dialogue

Edwin wasn't at all keen on the title, why couldn't it read: *In Conversation* rather than: *In Dialogue* ? But then he would laugh at himself, it had hardly been a conversation, more of a lecture, truth be told, and the photograph of himself taken the following sunny day, had turned out to be really rather handsome, he'd held it up again to the light.

Edwin Ray would also be invited to submit a design for the home of Charles Ore's widow, as would the Italian, Alessandro Cannizzaro. Gaia had always been fond of Italy and when Charles won a competition to build a museum there, she had very much hoped he'd suggest their moving in order to oversee the project, but alas no. Italy, was not for Charles.

Chapter Seven

Unwashed Pyjamas

Gaia moved the model opera house that usually straddled the bathtub onto the floor and turned the taps. Better put the plug in. Better move the model out of the bathroom completely, permanently, and not just for the duration of bathtime. It was now time for this room to be a bathroom. Nothing other. She poured in bath foam. Fragrant steam.

Still wearing socks.

These must be removed.

Trying to think, of simple, easy things, step by step.

Cigarette out.

Bath, in.

Ahhhh!

Gaia often spent time considering which her favourite room would be in a house that might be home. Bedroom and bathroom always in stiff competition. Right now it was bathroom.

Hot, the hotter the better. Draw out all that painful, stressful energy, then manage to sleep, like the dead – *no* – but sleep.

Sleep.

Spluttering, eyes stinging. Sleep... but not in the bath... *almost drowned fool woman*. Soapy waters reach sinus and save a life. Coughing, cold and shivery, curls lying lank; skin like shrivelled fruit. Surface scum floating. Rinse off quickly, hop out, rub dry.

The opera house resumed its natural place over the deep grimy valley. It had lived there too long to be relocated... and she liked it. Whatever else, she'd always admired Charles' work.

Tired and irritable, putting on the same-old unwashed pyjamas. It wasn't that the laundry didn't get done anymore, but lately it was way down low on the list of priorities, and was often just plain forgotten.

Cigarettes, and yes, whiskey. Time to write.

Letter: I hate him

Gaia to Selené

Dear Selené,

I hate him. I hate him so very much. *I HATE HIM!* Why, why secrets? His loyalty to you, well OK, but I was his wife. You and he seem to have shared such a beautiful friendship, why wouldn't he have wanted me to know about it?

Then the house. It seems he was finally designing his *perfect home*, perhaps this was intended for me and him but he wasn't sharing this with *me* but with *you, only you*. Oh you'll think I'm jealous, childish and I don't know what else, but think it damn you, think it! I hurt so much. I think it has passed a little, but then –

More than anything, I knew he didn't want children, that I can't deny, but I didn't know he'd done anything about it, I wasn't in on the snipping! Alright, he'd had it done before we even met, but he should have told me. Why oh why didn't he tell me, was it so unimportant, was I so unimportant?

I found out about you, and look what a fool I made of myself, and for what? Only to find it's a platonic relationship with a much older lady, someone I should have treated with so much more respect, someone who should have been invited to the funeral, you should have been at the funeral! He would have wanted you there. Look what the secrets have done, look what I have done!

I'm so desperately sorry, dear Selené, so sorry.

Gaia

Letter: Not running

Selené to Gaia

Dear Gaia,

Oh my dear, my dear, my dear! What wholesome anger, rage even. My sweet, it is but natural, and you must grieve. You must feel no guilt, but simply endure all the pain that is flying through, around and inside you – endure, embrace – My words might appear to be unkind ones, but their labour is in the service of your recovery. And to hide or try to escape life's pains never works, they follow, they catch you, if not at that moment, then later and more deeply. It is as though pains that are put off accrue interest and you are ultimately made to pay in ever greater amounts the longer you try to outwit or run from them. Be brave now. Face Charles' death, as indeed I believe you are in some measure. Yes, you are weak, but you are facing demons and not running from them. Not running. That is good. Ultimately you will become at ease again, and at readiness for pleasures – in time; but sweet you, not now.

You hate Charles, of course you do, and for now that is how you feel and how it has to be, be brave, face it, and do not run.

My love to you dear sweet Gaia.

Selené

Letter: You don't care

Gaia to Selené

Dear Selené,

Why, why do you never just answer my bloody questions? Why can't you just help me in a normal way? Why have I lost him? Why me? Why? Just help me, please.

Gaia

Letter: Just pain

Selené to Gaia

Dear Gaia,

'Normal', doesn't come into it, that is a term whose inference I am not interested in. 'Pain' however, is quite a different matter. Pain is something people strive so hard to push away, people think they might soar over it, build a new bridge or road and bypass it. Clichés darling, clichés. You can't. I have told you as much already, and you, Gaia, are no fool. Charles would not have shared his time with you had it been otherwise. Realise, your questions, your lambasting, is not something that needs a response. There are no answers to any of it. And as far as Charles, having lied, not told you certain things, good heavens! Does marriage give you rights to the contents of another's life in their entirety? Does marriage require the parties to give up the seeds, blossom and detritus of all the private, secret spaces in their heart, mind and soul? I see there are ever more reasons not to marry!

This will seem harsh, but I must say it to you, and you must take it on – Charles, and all that he did and didn't do, said and didn't, lied or didn't, kept secret or didn't, *is gone*. And there are no answers, solutions, nor are there conclusions.

Charles, sweet thing, is dead. He is dead.

The dogs are playing up, I shall walk them later till their poor legs fall from beneath them. God I need a sherry –

There, half a glass and I am much revived.

Gaia, it is not a question of fault. Strive to keep guilt, and a fear of punishment at bay, and *soldier on!* Pain must be made as welcome in your life as pleasure if you are ever to walk in step with your life. It is all about balance – emotional pain is no poor cousin to the physical kind, and most are dealt a fair – though seemingly unfair – amount of each. Where was I up to… oh yes, balance – when you fall from gladsome times, you land in a bed of anguish and affliction, and when the hurt has run itself out as it never fails to do, you are lifted again to more favourable dwellings. That's just how it is. So, you do as I say, and you might just be halfway alright.

So, no questions.

No guilt.

The sooner you welcome pain, the sooner it ups and leaves. Just look at how quickly pleasures end! The same can be true, at times, of pain. I do not underestimate your loss, I do not make light of your distress, but the faster you recognise pain as pain, and not as punishment, and stop searching for wretched explanations, the faster the pain finds its own level of register, and dissipates.

No matter how much we pollute this bountiful and cruel earth, the seas still move both in, and out. Keep breathing, keep breathing, and do not run.

Gaia, do not run. Hold fast.

Your strength

Selené

Letter: I will always hate him

Gaia to Selené

Dear Selené,

Why do I still feel I didn't know him? I read your letters but whilst I take on what you say, it is still only in a theoretical sense. I feel like the most worthless of students, all I want to do is push the same questions at you, I want to push *you*, almost as though I would hurt you physically, and now I am crying again. I could never harm anyone, and never ever you, you are an unimaginable strength to me, my lifeline. Your words are tough, but I trust your intention to be kind; and you show such wisdom to me, but I do not manage to put it into practice. I can't let go. I still feel the need for answers – that I might almost beat you for answers. – Why was he so often in the most awful of moods? Was he always that way? Was he that way when I first met him and I have since forgotten? Did he hide these parts of his character from me until we were married? His ego too, limitless! Perhaps I was responsible for his darker moods? Why was he always so intensely selfish, egocentric, secretive? WHY, I ask you, beg and would beat you, why?

Gaia

Whilst the first of this rally of letters was replied to almost on receipt, giving a delay generally of not more than a week, this last letter of Gaia's touched a nerve with Selené. The reply would take some time. It wasn't that she was offended, nor was it her own grief surfacing and overtaking, which indeed it may have, it was more a sense of helplessness seeping in. How ever she replied to the young widow now, it had to be powerful, and whatever else, it had to work – the responsibility was immense. Gaia was circling in on herself, and down. This next letter might be that which keeps the young woman alive.

Selené knew at least that Gaia would wait for this reply no matter how long it took. The widow had in essence placed her life in the older woman's hands. The hands of one she'd never even met. That level of vulnerability spoke volumes. That there was no one else she had turned to, no one else she felt she could or had wanted to rely on. No one else who'd be strong enough to help maintain her resolve not to take the pills she had collected and stored. She would go to the drawer of her dresser, roll one of the bottles across her palm, read part of the label as it moved – but tomorrow there might be another letter, or the next day, and in any case, the pills would still be there.

Selené took some three weeks to reply. In the meantime, Gaia read over the letters she'd received so far, sometimes finding just enough in one or other to help her 'hold fast', and if not, then ruminating on various reasons for the delayed response. Perhaps Tom was off work sick and the post office hadn't enough staff to cover his patch; or his kids were sick; or Selené was sick or on a trip somewhere, but she refused to think that Selené had given up on her. She was sure that Selené would reply. She ripped the cord from around the neck of one of the bottles, then shook it, not much sound, it was full, and that was good, if needed. She put the bottle back and closed the drawer.

The three weeks came around and so did Tom Bradshaw with his delivery. Gaia got up early, woken by worries, made frantic with sadness. She saw Tom from the window, she ran down and pulled open the door. It gave him a start.

"*Whoa*, steady, you gave me a bit of a fright there!"

Gaia didn't speak to him, neither did she look at him. Her eyes fixed directly on the stack of mail in his hand.

"Don't snatch! *Argh! You've... shit... you... you've drawn blood! Mrs Ore! Oh my! An' those aren't all for here...*"

She dropped the letters to the floor. Her gaze settling on the back of Tom's hand, deeply scratched. Women's nails made Tom nervous at the best of times. That was down to Cara, she had the talon type.

"How did you do that?" was now delivered by Gaia in a confusing mix of sincerity and astonishment as she considered the slim cuts and blood on the back of Tom's hand. Tom, totally perplexed, remained silent. This aggression was really out of character – he supposed. He was worried about the lady. Trying to make it look casual, he took a step back and with caution looked her over, he needed to make an assessment of things. Three months ago he'd seen her in pale slate pyjamas, now she was in dark slate pyjamas. Were they the same ones? *Jesus!* He stole a quick look into the house. It seemed quite dark inside, but from what he could make out, it didn't appear too friendly on the hygiene front. "How did you do that?" she said again.

"How did I do that? *How did I do that?!*" The line had finally needled him, "You did it! Just this minute. How did *I* do it ?!"

She felt she partly remembered, but wasn't entirely sure, things seemed foggy, "I did? I did, oh, oh," and she went to take the injured hand in both of hers, and tenderly so, but he jerked his arm back and his hand out of harm's reach.

"And like I said, *Mrs Ore*, those aren't all for you, if you had a little bit of patience, I was just separating yours as I came up the steps. I know you're, you're still in, what–d'ya–call–it... mour... mournin' but just *slowww* down some, slow it all up, yeah? Calm there now." The last, revealing the compassionate self that made up much of Tom Bradshaw. Gaia, was tongue-tied; she remained still now for fear of inflicting further unintentional injury.

Tom backed away a little further, then marking where she stood with a stern look, he courageously gathered up the floored mail. He shuffled through it.

"You could come in."

Tom looked startled, "*No way!*... I mean, oh, no, but thank you." He put on a smile, a half smile, "Actually, only this one for you after all that... palaver."

Gaia's transfusion had arrived.

Letter: Testy characters

Selené to Gaia

Dear Gaia,

I am not yours nor anyone's 'lifeline'. Heaven forbid. Each must be his own. I am not insulted, but nor am I flattered.

I move strength towards you, all you have to do is move with it.

Now then, I will make some things plain to you and then you must let go of them.

With regard to Charles, there are certain things that have to be taken into consideration, and certain things that you have to realise. One of these is that his mother had both a very forceful and a very indulgent nature. She was a curious being. Best not examined too closely, I always thought. I nurture no great fondness for mothers. Mothers! Terrible things largely. Such an important role and one to which so few are suited. Certainly not me, hence my vowing never to become one. Self-hate, how wretched might that be?

What I am trying to say is that I don't really understand why, during your marriage, you seem so surprised by certain aspects of Charles' character. Aspects, which as far as I can see, even he, talented as he was at so many things, soon master at almost anything he set his mind to – *no, Gaia* – even he wouldn't have been able to subdue and certainly not hide his being wilful, headstrong. I would go as far as to say that he was a man with an almost obedient reaction to his own thoughts and desires. One can only be thankful that these were never of too mean nor cruel a nature. He was always a gentle man, if he was never a gentleman. And to my knowledge, he was never one to waste time on self-analysis, let alone criticism. He simply was who he was, *Charles!* I make no attempt to defend the more testy aspects of his character, and Lord knows there were many. But Gaia darling, don't you see? This was a man suckled on breasts with: WILL TO POWER tattooed across them! *What did you expect?!*

Now let that be enough! An end to the berating, of me, of him, and most importantly of yourself! It has become almost bullying, be careful, I will not tolerate more.

My love

Selené

Chapter Eight
Scratch Card–Lucky

Somehow or other Tom now felt, if not compelled, then at least as duty bound as he was already toward the widow of Charles Ore, and so, in some small way he wanted to help, wanted to cheer her up. He didn't know how he would do this, but he suspected it would require a bit of cash. In Tom's experience, cheering up womenfolk usually cost money. Cara took care of the money, all the money, and spare cash just didn't exist. So finding *extra* cash, well this was going to take some luck. And whilst waiting for this windfall, Tom ruminated on what he would do with it. Hell, if a woman *will* wear pyjamas, she might at least wear nice new ones!

The following week Tom hit lucky with a scratch card. It wasn't strictly speaking *his* scratch card, but come on, Cara had so many, she wouldn't miss just one, and anyway, why should she get to have all the fun?

"Beginner's luck? Well, it's gotta happen to someone, might as well be me!" Tom beamed.

The kids didn't really need anything and Cara had clothes enough to dress a street carnival. One of those big out-of-control carnivals that started off community based and friendly but now attracted two-hundred-and-fifty-thousand, and they just kept coming back – minus the few that got killed each year. Tom hated how easily that stuff happened, specially since he'd had kids, specially since he'd lost one, and his dog had had to die too. Stupid dog. – He thumbed through one of Cara's catalogues while she was sleeping – that looked about right – but maybe the widow was a size smaller than Cara. He checked through some of Cara's stuff for sizes. It occurred to him just to swipe something of hers, but she'd notice, besides, Cara didn't wear pyjamas. You didn't get a big family by wearing pyjamas! Looking at the catalogue, he settled for a rose-coloured pair, thinking the colour was cheerful, hoping that might help bring Mrs Ore back to a *rosier* mood, he smiled. Yeah, a size smaller than Cara, he filled out the boxes and ordered. This was kinda fun, first time scratch card user becomes first time winner, and a natural at catalogue shopping. He took a proud deep breath. When he could get round to saving for a computer, he was sure to be a natural at internet shopping too – There'll be no stopping me, he beamed. He put his friend's address down on the order sheet – because shit, if Cara knew about it, he'd never explain it wasn't *another* woman, and only the skinny Architect's widow who he felt he *sort of, ought to, kind of* help out – he and Charles had been on first name terms after all. No, that wouldn't wash with a woman like Cara.

Service is improving these days, he thought, all pleased as his friend called to say the parcel had arrived in the 'twenty-four hours after receipt of order' just as it had said on the page. Cool!

Now all he had to do was figure out how to give this *vaguely-confused-bereaved… and possibly 'coming-onto-him'* kind of woman a pair of rose-coloured pyjamas. – Suddenly he wasn't sure this was such a great idea. Um…. He'd think it over. He removed all the packaging and shook out the pyjamas, yeah, good choice, should suit her nice. A bit brighter than her misery-jamas at any rate. Poor Charles! No wonder they never had any little ones. Always wondered, she's an attractive woman when all's said and done, in an ordinary sort of way, but wholesome enough, bit small round the hips maybe but alright mostly. Rose, no rose was definitely better than grey, if they insist on wearing something in bed. Nothing so off-putting as pond-water-grey – but should he really be giving her a gift at all?

Finally, his altruism got the better of him. He'd do it alright, he'd give her the rosy-jamas. But first he hid them in his locker at work, allowing himself a day or two to work out how to do it. The right way to do it. He was, however, starting to realise that this spontaneous act of kindness might get him into all kinds of trouble if he didn't handle it – just right.

As was often the case, Tom had grossly underestimated Cara, who kept a holy-watch over her scratch card investments. He didn't know it yet, but boy he had it coming to him.

Next morning, he was to deliver a letter of condolence from Italian architect Alessandro Cannizzaro. Cute stamps, fancy handwriting, another artist-type he assumed. The envelope had come undone. Tom had never done this before, though often tempted; he knew it was illegal, he could lose his job and more, but somehow – this time, the letter slipped from its wrapping and found itself laid open between his thick thumbs and itching fingers. Rain began to drum on the back of his cap in fat droplets, the adrenalin kicked in. He leant under the Construct's overhang to protect the ink and hand-made paper.

Letter: From Italy

Alessandro Cannizzaro to Gaia

Dear Mrs Ore,

Please forgive me for not writing to you sooner, but perhaps you have already been drowning in letters of sorrow, and I would rather try to raise the spirit. Of course in the first place I give you my deepest sympathy. Charles Ore is also a very great loss to the world of architecture, and as one of his contemporaries I have to say he had many qualities to admire, perhaps even to envy. What can I say, he even beat me to the design of a great museum in my own country! What a man! And I will say – though as a competitor you will appreciate that it is painful to do so – that his design was truly remarkable.

I'm looking at a photograph of each of you in a magazine – I never had the opportunity to meet with either of you, and that I deeply regret.

Forgive me if this disturbs you in any way, but I hope not, and please – if you need some time in a completely different atmosphere, different surroundings, know that I would feel so honoured if you would visit Italy. If you needed to be alone, I would arrange that, and if not, I hope you would allow me to be your host. Take your time to decide, the offer will always remain open.

Yours

Alessandro

Wow! What a nice guy, what a nice friend to have. The man hadn't even met the widow. Tom felt overcome. That someone could show so much emotion and damned kindness to another someone that they hadn't even met, that was too nice. He wiped away an escaping tear, and then panicked as he noticed that he'd now added a dirty thumbprint to the edge of the page. Quickly he folded it up and put it back in the envelope. He took out his notepad and copied down the name and address of the sender printed at the edge. Right now he wasn't sure why he did this, but he felt he needed to keep open the possibility of *something,* just in case. Just in case what? Well, just in case. Then taking a moment to compose himself, he pushed Alessandro through Gaia's door along with the phone bill and her share of junk mail.

Tom finished off his round and wended his way back through grey streets and greyer rain. He fell into one of his TV career fantasises, this particular one was his meteorological fantasy – *Tom Bradshaw, Weather Man.* Rain had got big and fat of late and *way*-heavy, and *way*-torrential. He loved how the real TV guy had taken to calling it the Metropolitan Monsoon. He was a cool guy, Tom used him as his weatherman-role model. Monsooooon, *achew!* He sneezed his Metropolitan mailbag along with his Metropolitan self, back to home base, and his locker. Without having given conscious thought to it – *Eureka!* – he'd suddenly worked out how to give Gaia the rosy-jamas. That was it, he'd wait a while, couple of weeks or so, wrap 'em up nice, and send them from the nice guy, from Alessandro, hell, that's exactly the sort of thing a sweet guy like that would do. He smiled, big.

Back at home, scratch-card-queen Cara is missing a scratch card. She isn't smiling, big or otherwise, she isn't happy. When she finds out who's taken her scratch card, she's gonna mince 'em. If she finds out it was a winning card, she'll mince 'em real good. If she finds out it was a winning card and the money's gone, well then… she'll mince 'em, fry 'em and eat 'em!

Chapter Nine
Alessandro Cannizzaro

Alessandro Cannizzaro was one of those enviable characters who despite appearing to bear all the traits of a thoroughly nauseating egomaniac, was somehow almost completely adorable. His vanity, whilst gargantuan, contained elements of humour that allowed many to forgive him; and beyond that he was amongst other things, a great physical beauty. What the Greeks had attributed their gods, the gods themselves bestowed aplenty on the Italian, Alessandro. That was in itself reason enough for other men to resent, even despise him, but then he was also a star in the world of architecture, a star, and a shining one.

As a child Alessandro quickly realised how much he could get away with.

"Who did it, who did it?" the four-year-old's mother screamed. She had been baking half the night, since before the warm morning sun had even thought to rouse itself. The whole family were coming, the uncles, the aunts, cousins, second and third cousins; Maria had a feast to prepare, and someone had stolen half her bounty. Home-made breads were her speciality. She ran about the streets scolding the children of friends and neighbours, the lazy husband of a former friend, the sky, the stars and heaven above. Meanwhile, a little boy was piling up the baking treasure in his 'materials box', ordering the breads by size, shape and weight. Some, he had already begun to cut and carve into shape in preparation for assembly, but before that he needed to work out the proportions of flour to water with which to cement the parts together. The results from the practice batch were fairly brittle, but if handled carefully, the main structures might last out the summer. From the attic, he could hear his mother's screeching as it swirled around the house, the streets, through open windows, under the doors, and quavering through the hairs on the dog's back. The dog, Corbusier, twitched his ears and shoulders trying to shake the

sound away. To Alessandro, the words were a blur, simply jolting into one another, linked only by the consistent howl of a frantic mother. Why it hadn't occurred to her to look closer to home for the culprit could not be understood, her husband speculated that she enjoyed the excuse to rant at various neighbours and particular friends, and that she needed the exercise, physically, vocally and emotionally. He never took Maria's outbursts too seriously, and was never surprised that little Alessandro was usually the cause. Whatever was behind Alessandro's mischief usually entertained his father quite well. He had noticed something special in the boy from the moment of his birth. An energy. A vitality. Something otherworldly. Something he hadn't seen in any of the others. Alessandro had two elder sisters, and three moody, hapless elder brothers. Little Alessandro was sure his three brothers were connected at the hips, and were not really human but some fantastic Greek mythological creature yet to be named.

Later, aged five, he decided that the brothers were a blend of the three basic forms of classical Greek architecture, Doric, Corinthian and Ionic, and that as one mythological creature they combined to be known as: Dorkion, thus he addressed each of them, whether in the plural or singular from then on. He did think the eldest to be the ugliest and most horrid and therefore he must surely be the Corinthian, that being the most ornate and in Alessandro's estimation, the most hateful.

When Bread City was discovered several hours later, mother Maria was quite overcome. Everyone was summoned. The brothers rolled their evil eyes, awaiting Alessandro's comeuppance. "Come and look, Papa," Maria called down to her husband, "Look what he has done! Oh Alessandro, you beautiful, beautiful boy! You love your mama's cooking so much, you build your own little world from it! Look at these towers, these walls, oh my darling darling boy! Our very own Giotto!" She smothered him with kisses as the brothers gritted their teeth, meanly slitting their eyes, ever amazed at how much the small demon could get away with.

Inhabiting Alessandro's model world in bread, were penguins, tiny, wooden, hand-carved penguins. For penguins were funny, and penguins appeared, perhaps more than many creatures, humans in particular, to walk at exactly the right pace, in step with their world. Not too fast, nor too slow. He had no idea that this would later flower into theories of harmonious dwelling, but so it was.

Alessandro's gathering intelligence did not play shadow to his good looks for long, and anything his looks alone did not elicit, his intellect, talent and childlike humour surely did. Ebullient human notes combined in wild rhythms. Alessandro, an intoxicating spirit of passions.

As a student of architecture, one of his professors – and indeed, lovers – was to remark, "Alessandro, you're one hell of a human cocktail." The American professor was called Simone, Simone Divine, a name that made Alessandro swoon – irreverently. He nicknamed her: *The Divine*. "Never take a woman too seriously – that I learned from my father – it always keeps them on their toes, their tip-tippy-toes, where they should be, like ballerinas, suffering whilst elegantly reaching up for your attention, trying to hold on to some semblance of serenity." Their paths crossed by chance some years later when Alessandro's works were winning ever more prestigious competitions. They shared a bottle of Sauvignon Blanc – "The French, they have a talent for quite a few things, ah!" – he began to update the Divine on how it is to be Italy's finest. He would have taken her again to bed, but for what? She had nurtured many grand ideas in that regard, and how much had she missed him, but for Alessandro, that had run its course. There was nothing further to be experienced with her.

Alessandro had never meant to snub those he had loved… but after a time there were simply too many. Men also adored him sexually, but only ever from a distance, his insatiability was for women, and many a young man had wept.

When the time came, Alessandro would clearly be delighted to compete in a competition to design for the ethereal and enigmatic Gaia. An architect's clients are many things, but rarely so subtly enchanting.

Letter: In Recovery
Gaia to Selené

Dear Selené,

I hardly knew how to reply to you, and that is the reason for the delay. Your last letter, though frightening almost, was exactly the one needed. It can't have been easy for you, and I have to remember that you are also bereaved. I have a deep respect for you, and thank you for not abandoning me. Enough, I must not stray into yet more sentimentality.

I wanted to tell you about something curious that happened recently, I expect you might find it amusing, but I'm still not sure what to make of it myself. Some weeks ago I received a letter of sympathy from another of Charles' peers in the ranks of the architectural elite, one Alessandro Cannizzaro. I am certain you will have heard of him. The letter went on to invite me to Italy though he's never met either Charles or myself. I longed to move to Italy when Charles won the museum commission, but Italy and Italians were never really Charles' taste. The invitation isn't the most shocking part. Three weeks later I received a parcel from him, though not exactly from Italy, as the gift was from this country and the stamps and postal marks were missing, but he'd sent me pyjamas! Rose-pink pyjamas! Now what do you make of that? Is that not completely eccentric, mad even? It makes me laugh, but isn't it strange? What's more, they fit! I ought not to complain, even our local mailman commented on my 'rosy-jamas' as he called them (I opened the door to him in them one morning, I needed to thank him for his kindness when I first lost Charles and to apologise for having accidentally scratched him — don't ask, it's too embarrassing, sometimes I think bereavement is a form of insanity.) Anyway, the mailman said that the pink pyjamas made me look more cheerful, and that he was sure that would be what Charles wanted. I still find it rather peculiar. Any ideas, oh wise one?

Very much love

Gaia

Alessandro soon received a letter of thanks for the pyjamas which Gaia shyly described as 'the gift'. He paced up and down, her letter in one hand, a cigarette in the other, trying to make sense of the widow's words, trying to imagine the voice that belonged to the beguiling picture of her in the magazine. Gucci shirt, simple and sexy – but really she would look gorgeous in anything. The article, a full length feature on:

The late Charles Ore, his Work and his Life

Alessandro looked again at the magazine, the page, her picture, he smiled. With such a woman in your life it should at least have been titled:

The Architect, his Work and his 'Wife'!

In the magazine Charles exudes smug self-approval surrounded by his plans, whilst Gaia looks elegant… but lost. Alessandro wished she looked less nervous, less lonely, and he thinks frivolously that perhaps he would make her a better husband.

In an attempt to feel closer to the widow, he switches to thinking, for the moment, in English, drops the magazine and takes up the letter again, waltzing about the room alone, somewhat seduced by what he imagines her to be.

These foreigners can be quite funny, why does she thank me for a gift? Did I send something to her? No. I think she is English, and they can be quite strange, I've noticed that before. – How cute, all I have sent her is a letter, just a little letter, but for her it is a 'gift'. Quite modest, quite sweet, but woman, it was just a letter. Yet if I have given her so much pleasure from almost nothing, well, that makes me a very happy man. And she, so grateful, so quick to take pleasure in such a very small thing, well I think she must be a woman of open and warm heart, maybe she is something like myself? Who knows, anyway, that's nice, really nice. But no mention of a visit, it is too early yet for such things. Of course. Maybe… I wait a little while, and ask her again.

Letter: From the Lifeline

Selené to Gaia

Dear sweet Gaia,

I can feel a kind of gaiety arising in you, how heartening. And whatever you do, do not stray into feelings of guilt. It is very good progress to sense in you, what shall I call it? A sign, yes a sign that you will certainly recover. It won't be quick, it is barely six months, and at times you must expect to fall back, in fact I am sure you will, but expect it and do not be afraid. It seems you might well be over the worst. What a wonderful spirit you have. I believe yours is a healing spirit, and a healing spirit is also one easily healed, my dear.

Now then, the Italian, yes I have indeed heard of him. A very great rival of Charles', somewhat younger than him; certainly of the same order and calibre if such is possible. He's sent you pyjamas! Marvellous! Men, such funny things.

It seems rather inappropriate at present, and so I cannot allow myself to tell you of my most recent lover. Perhaps another time.

Write soon, eat well, and take care of your health, I must get on just now.

My love to you

Selené

Letter: To one too Old

Gaia to Selené

Dear Selené,

Your letter really made me laugh, you speak of having a lover! I looked back at one of the last three letters you sent to my dear Charles, one in which you actually talk of *taking a new lover*, and mention how *freshly cut grass* arouses you *more than the scent of any man*! I realise now, that you often speak in codes, and just as the *little ones* were not children but your spaniels, *lover* is obviously code for something else. I'm no good at puzzles, so you must forgive me as I cannot make it out. Hilarious though to imagine a misanthropic intellectual over seventy with a troop of King Charles spaniels, taking lovers! How mad! Forgive me. Anyway, I hope you will enlighten.

Then I have to complain a little as you barely commented at all on the Italian having sent me a gift. I did write to thank him.

Do you think we could meet? I would so love to meet you, I don't have any false hopes of replacing Charles in your affection, but feel the closeness you so generously spoke of in our early correspondence.

My very best wishes and love

Gaia

Gaia could not work out why this should be, but Selené took six full weeks to reply, giving in only after Gaia had sent a further three notes begging to know what was amiss, enquiring after Selené's health and finally the health of six King Charles spaniels.

Letter: To the Ignorant

Selené to Gaia

Dear Gaia,

The dogs' and my health are all fine, thank you.

Little fool you, insolent little fool! Your letter did rile me I can tell you. Still, it is interesting for me to learn more of your character, and goodness me, girl, how have you lasted this long in the world quite that naïve? Beyond me!

Again I am made to spell something out to you. Vexed, I am. LOVERS of mine, madam, are exactly that and no damn metaphor. Do you think that my seniority in years makes me dead all over? On what do you base such assumptions, pray? Goodness gracious me! Are you gone quite mad? Though the companionship of neither man nor woman can generally offer me anything I might find useful, there are still desires in this soul, and of this body, whose thirst for life, poetry and even grit, are deliciously and gainfully sought and met.

Now that I have that off my chest, I shall take a sherry and a break, and then add a few more lines, though you don't deserve them.

Half a bloody bottle! I hope you're happy. I am. No I must not go overboard with you, and my humour is something you haven't yet quite understood. I had intended, but indeed forgot to add in my last letter, that perhaps a stint in Italy would do you a power of good. Tell me, when Charles was alive, did you ever do what you want? Do you ever do what you want?

As for visiting me, darling you must not take this unkindly, but really no. I do so like my life the way it is. Don't come. This has no bearing on your recent foolish correspondence, but really I just know what suits me. I know you'll find that hard to take. I'll look out some photographs, the dogs and suchlike to show there's no hard feeling. I can't do it now but will send them on another time.

I was actually thinking that perhaps you should take that postman to bed, if he is so enamoured! Sex, darling, a very underestimated medicine in my book. Don't be shocked, or indeed 'do' be shocked, it's jolly well time you were. Time, sweet Gaia, to wake up.

My warmest affection with this short sharp slap

Selené

Chapter Ten
Monroe-kissable

Cara was more than a size bigger than Gaia, she just liked to wear things clingy. Cara was BIG, bigger than Tom for sure, and with all the kids and the fetching and carrying for them, she was pretty strong too. She ran on a short fuse, and it seems fair to say, that when she decided to bite, she had too much in common with a certain dog they once owned. Tom, a two pit bull man. That possibly made him a too stupid man, but stupid or not, most couldn't help but like him.

Cara continued looking for her missing scratch card, and looking turned to searching, and soon the touch paper was lit. She took to hollering, cushion bashing, magazine hurling and soundwave abusing. Tom was lucky. He wasn't home.

Her pretty green eyes sparkled, her pupils pin-pricks and homing in on every surface. She clawed her pinky stuck on-nails through the living room waste paper basket, down the sides of the sofa, through her tangled angry hair. Her hair was pretty when she brushed it, she was, all told, pretty, except when she was mad, "Pretty all over, that's my Cara, it's just about the only word that'll do. Pretty," Tom would say, "except when she was mad."

"If we still had that dumb dog, I'd swear it was him that'd stolen and chewed up my card." Cara, was looking for clues, first removing certain creatures from the frame of suspicion and fine-tuning the list of possible suspects. Two nails had been sacrificed in the search and this clearly upped the ante. The kids couldn't be included in the investigations. The kids knew better.

Tom sauntered up the pathway, whistling. Cara hated whistling. She put on some music in an attempt to cool down a little. She scanned the list of tunes, her anger management self-help book advised on choosing something light and cheery that would encourage a change of mood. Tom Jones, that was it, over the top, old fashioned groove, that might just do it. She selected the playing order of the tracks, her breathing coming under more control. 'This and That' was the first track, and she slowly let her shoulders roll around, as though some great hunk was massaging them. Hips swaying, she sang along with the lyrics. As her husband reached the front door and stepped inside she'd just reached the chorus, her favourite part.

Ooh I've had e-nough of this and that, and this and that is no good!
I said, I've had e-nough of this and that, and this and that is no good!

These last words, and catching sight of poor Tom, were just what was required to rev that woman's anger-engine. She snarled. He spoke, "Wow, I never seen old Jonesy work that into his routine, makes you look kinda mean, Cara. You're far too pretty for that."

She turned and fixed her sight on him. Homing in on the target. Two nails down, she could do less damage than with a full set but she could still do plenty.

"What's up, Cara? You having a bad day, babe?"

"When you 'babe' me, it's always a sure sign you're behind what's bugging me. You took my scratch card didn't you, *DIDN'T YOU?*" Tom Jones had run on:

More than the greatest love the world has ever known
This – is the love I'll give – to you alone…

Tom Bradshaw's big mistake here was to think he might serenade her out of this killer mood. He tried to work in a few dance moves. Unfortunately for him the track jumped to 'Ten Guitars'. Cara yelled over both Toms and took a firm grip of her husband's pride and joy guitar. She smiled cunningly, lifting the guitar and swirling it high above her head, slowly, carefully, at first.

Dance, dance, dance to my ten guitars…

Tom turned on his heel to witness his 'other love' being rotated like a helicopter blade. He froze, one foot still mid-air. Now she froze. The 'other love' held captive overhead. Her features softened, the power, all hers. The adrenalin was fed like it had been injected, full speed, and she was buzzing. Nervously Tom enquired, "You alright? You looked real sexy, singing and swaying as I walked in." Silence, no words at all, the music ran out, just the hum of traffic up and down the street outside. Tom began to stammer, "Somethin… on you-r mind? Aren't you gonna say something, babe?"

"I already said, and you know exactly what's on *my mind*, and if you don't own up right soon, this guitar is gonna be on yours." She licked her bottom lip. She had gorgeous, plump sweetheart lips, Monroe-kissable Tom called them, though he didn't much fancy his chances with such comparisons right now. It was weird though, she was so angry, there was his guitar about to be smashed to smithereens, and yet he felt strangely turned on by the whole scene. Hormones, he thought, really dumb things at times. *Stop thinking about sex, she's about to destroy my gui-tar, hell!* Fortunately his instincts told him that wiggling his own hips and a few verses of 'Dr. Love' weren't going to get him out of this one, and he had sense enough to remain still.

"Yes it was me," he said, as though confessing to murder.

A day later it turned out that their neighbour, Myrtle, head of the neighbourhood watch team, god-bless-her, had witnessed Tom taking the scratch card to collect his winnings, Tom was then doubly pleased that he'd so quickly chosen the route of confession. He did manage to get away with a partial lie. He said he'd taken the card at a moment of weakness, which was something Cara could relate to, she was often subject to the same, but he shrunk the amount of his winnings to the second lowest possible, hoping against hope that the tenacious, tentacled Myrtle hadn't had him under too close a surveillance the whole time. Did that woman have nothing else to do? Cara accepted the slightly forced-out-of-him confession and took the amount as truth, saying he owed her the same plus the cost of an entire new set of nails. Ouch! That false stuff is pricey, but a lot more pain and guitar abuse may have come his way, and he knew he'd got off lightly. *Phew!* The admission also resulted in the surprising sexual gratitude of the Monroe-kissable; hey, every cloud!

"Well Tom, I'm really proud that you didn't try and deny it. You're a good boy mostly, just I have to keep an eye on you." Cara was younger than Tom, though nobody would guess it. She sat on his lap running her fingers through his hair, playing now with her other favourite lyrics, as sung by the kissable:

...it is naughty, but then
Oh... do it again,
Ple-ase, do it again.

She sounded nothing like Monroe, but he could shush her gently, and when he half closed his eyes, she sure felt like her.

Chapter Eleven
What Counts

Charles Ore had always sought to learn as much as his brain could possibly hold. As a child it was evident that he had both a photographic memory and a very active visual imagination. One of his earliest obsessions lay with maps, and for a while he was entirely devoted to exactly that: considering longitudes and latitudes, imposing new gridlines, a touch of realignment here and there, redrawing boundaries, contemplating fixed and moveable points. A spot of global management, one might say. To Selené's mind, Charles was the kind of child who should be actively discouraged from a career in politics.

Charles was a brilliant, if eccentric little boy and his desire for knowledge was insatiable: all knowledge, though particularly of mathematics and art. It was as though the role of architect lay waiting for him. Selené had been relieved by this, finding architecture the lesser of several evils, once remarking, "There are three careers that seem to have been prepared for the egomaniac: Politics, Parenting, and Architecture!" In his adult years, Charles would certainly come to agree with her — with regard at least, to the first two. In his early teens, he avidly pursued an interest in building design, in structure, and process. His emotional development however, came a poor second to the intellectual, and his inability to recognise the types of behaviour generally considered acceptable or preferable, was quite impaired. This landed him in trouble. Much of the time, he could explain his way out of things when faults were levelled at him, or else his doting parents would romance him out of bother. It was often easy to forgive the gifted boy, but over time, he became less inclined to explain, and threads of arrogance began to find root. If people were too stupid to realise the importance of his research, his interests, then young Charles had no time to explain. At thirteen he rather aggressively and pompously exclaimed, "Mother, as the Chinese would say,: *It is like playing the violin to a cow!*" The mother, too easily amused, watered the roots, and the father provided manure, ensuring virulent growth, "Quite right my boy, there's no educating fools!" Charles was an only child; Hermoine and Henrik, his only parents. If it had not been for the occasional interventions of a certain *not-even-blood-related sort of aunt*, things could arguably have been worse.

Evil's Folly...

At the sweet and tender age of nine, Charles embarked on what most would term: *breaking and entering*. To Charles, intellectual acrobatics and the pursuit of knowledge could not be fettered by petty matters such as ownership of property, seeking permission, respecting privacy, damage to said property, or the nerves of old ladies.

At around eleven o'clock one adrenalin-soaked evening, a determined young Charles ventured out on an analytical architectural MISSION. Evelyn Dawn, secretly nicknamed Evil-in by Charles, was deep in slumber. She was well over eighty and lived, Charles presumed, alone. She had enjoyed her nightcap and taken to her bed shortly after nine. Evelyn Dawn lived in an old enchanted folly; it was easy to see why children found it fascinating, but the rumours of witchery were sufficient to keep most small demons at bay.

Charles decided to break into the ancient folly through one of its numerous dark-paned windows. This one was tantalisingly high up. He shone his lengthy, narrow-beamed torch upwards, feeling the buzz of his adventure. This magical folly had been the subject of intense interest to Charles since he was small, and now he was 'big' he was actually entering the bewitching dwelling, now he would get things answered, test out his structural hypotheses.

Evil's Folly... just how was that building constructed? It wasn't easy to tell from the outside. Charles had trailed around it dozens of times looking for clues, and once even managed to roam about the roof, but alas, nothing. So it had to be done. He'd simply had to go in. It never occurred to Charles to ask anyone, see if his parents might arrange a visit, a look around, for where would the fun have been in that? Besides, she was Evil-in and would never have permitted it, of that he was sure. It was also an adventure, the type of thing that young men have to accomplish entirely by themselves, otherwise – *it simply doesn't count!*

Having levered open the window, one set at quite a ridiculous angle (he was beginning to regret having chosen this one), he perched some moments on the ledge, his heart pounding viciously. It might explode. He must slow that breathing, calm a little lest he hyperventilate. Missions cannot be ruined before they are hardly even begun! He made a mental note about that, and just as he did he lost his balance. He wavered, almost out, then overcompensating and falling inwards and with too much speed. Wow! That was completely disconcerting, the floor should never have been that far down! He dropped and dropped and when he did hit the floor it shot up through him with a judder. A painful, ankle-twisting, neck-jerking judder. He'd managed to keep hold of the torch, but in adjusting to the light, the dark had tricked him. He bashed the torch on the ground in anger, and now it would keep cutting out on him. Pride comes at a price, especially aged nine. The problem wasn't that the torch-bashing woke Evil-in, she was half deaf, the problem *waa-aas…* that it disturbed her cat, who wasn't.

Now Charles, whilst for the most part fearless, *was* deeply afraid of all things feline: tigers, jaguars, panthers, and worst of all, DOMESTIC CATS! Gigi bounded down the stone stairwell and stealthily swung herself into the dug-out basement that contained the intruder, *Meeeeow!* Gigi peered sideways, then slowly, like a search light, looked deep across the room. Green eyes. Charles had frozen in position, pins and needles in one arm, cramp developing in the other, and legs, possibly broken. He took out his notebook and made a quick reconnoitre: stuck in enemy territory, sustained probable permanent injury, unarmed, and now being circled by THE ENEMY'S TROOPS (there might well be more hiding in the shadows… as back up!). Unfortunately there was nothing written into the rule book that said a child genius would be blessed with decent battle skills. If he kept still, she might not see him, but his eyes soon betrayed his position, and in the slightest of movements she'd got him. Now they were eyeball to eyeball, and Gigi had her prey.

Her hips swayed, her body rippled, her thick fur coat proudly adorning; her sultry eyelashes whipping the stilled atmosphere. Charles felt her presence digest all the oxygen, he couldn't breathe. Her eyes changed colour, her pupils changed shape, the room span around. His head fell and his body crumpled to meet his shortened zigzagged legs.

When Charles came round, his legs weren't broken, his body wasn't tied to a rack, nor was Gigi the sabre-tooth that she had taken the shape of during his dream, but curiously, he was now wearing a hat, a rather weighty, rather warm… hat. Without moving, he peered from side to side and up and around, no enemy, phew! Then a tickle in his ear alerted him to his hat, but he didn't have a hat, he had never owned a hat. Gigi purred, her tail tickling his ear and the side of his neck, she sat proudly on the head of her prey. She stretched a paw out straight and tweaked the purple air with her talons. The tightness in his chest returned. He needed to breathe, needed to move, throw off this creature, keep focused on the mission, for this was a MISSION after all! One, grasped, and deep as he could muster, breath, and he leapt to his feet. Gigi fled, clawing his cheek as she went. His legs felt crushed, his ankles were twisted but he shot up and onto a ledge in sheer determination. There! He took some moments to breathe properly and reassess. The notebook re-emerged, OK: penetrated enemy territory, tick: goal achieved; maintaining position behind enemy lines, tick: goal achieved; encountered sabre-tooth tiger, proved to be quite an obstacle, fought and outwitted sabre-tooth, tick: goal achieved; incurred injuries – this is a setback but adds to the challenge, must not give up! Important: main enemy not alerted, main objective still intact and possible to achieve, achievement of main goal *despite injury*, will – enhance mission success! Must move on!

Charles gave his legs a quick rub, but decided that the pain and discomfort would simply have to be ignored! He had to be a man. He pulled himself up almost straight, being a man is a tough business, he thought, a tear in the corner of his eye.

He realised that the ledge he was now on formed part of a series, and where he had fallen from the window was a deep shaft into a dugout room. The terracing itself seemed to have no purpose, a physical joke almost. The shaft made sense in as much as it might simply have been a trap for burglars, a dropped void, quite sensible in Charles' estimation despite having fallen victim to it himself. But not for a second did it occur to him that he may appear to be a burglar, and as he certainly had no intention of taking anything, such an interpretation would have been entirely lost on him. He scrambled from one ledge to the next, trying to assign functions to them whilst aiming for a door to the side of one further up.

Gigi, meantime, was most offended by the disruptive behaviour of her captive. She licked her claw, boy's blood! Too sweet. She shook out her coat in disgust, then set off to alert her companion, the eminent Evelyn Dawn, to the presence of the intruder.

Charles pushed at the wooden door, moving about slowly, noting structural details as he went along but straining to see clearly, the torch was still playing up, and his head still felt fuzzy. The folly seemed so much bigger on the inside, mysterious, cavernous!

Gigi puffed out her chest and swaggered into her companion's chamber. She jumped onto the bed. She clawed a little at the embroidery on the bedspread, she'd never liked that fussy floral stitching, she'd have a good go at it another day. Now, for the job at hand, first step: wake the woman. She curled herself around Evelyn Dawn's head, and firmly held her tail moustachioed across the face, closing up the nostrils. Cut their breathing and they wake in no time, if they're not dead already. Gigi had had that happen once, with a previous companion.

A shot of brandy before bedtime, two hours or so of deep blissful slumber in ample feathered heaven, and the swift curtailment of one's breathing. WHAT! Dragging in breath, inhaling nought but musty fur. Execution! No! Gigi suddenly realised her heavy-tail-ed-ness was about to reap the wrong reward. She whipped her fluffy tail out of the way and slunk some distance away on the bed, worried, watching. ACHEW! The sneeze was a veritable tsunami.

ACHEW! ACHEW! ACHEW! A monumental sneezing attack, but the best defence really, Gigi was most familiar with the effects of a stuck fur ball. She was glad the companion could so strenuously clear her airwaves, her guilt subsided. There was a job to be done!

The sneezing echoed through the folly, sometimes doubling back on itself so that the direction from which it originated could not easily be discerned. Charles shook his head to clear his ears. What on earth was that? Again and again and again! He wasn't sure he wanted to find out. He continued with his notes on matters architectural and tried not to be unnerved by the various disembodied yowls. Oh, why did Evil-in have to have a cat? But perhaps it made sense, she being a witch and all. Charles however, much preferred dogs. Nice women keep dogs, like aunt Selené, yes that was it! Nice women keep dogs, witches keep cats.

He felt the deep scratch on his face, the blood had dried quickly, it was a tough lot, but there it was, this MISSION simply had to be accomplished. And now he had a pocketbook full of notes and drawings, several new queries; undoubtedly great bruises; pulled and possibly torn ligaments; and a full-on battle with a sabre-tooth, all under his belt. What a night's work! Almost done!

The old lady decided on a shortcut using the hidden door through the small horticulture library. Across the small room, Charles suspected his eyes were playing tricks, the books moved, then a whole set of shelves from floor to ceiling seemed to move. The torch failed again. His breathing increased, he shook his head, and closed his eyes to rest them a moment, hoping to open them to books that were not moving. The lids went up, and there before him was the famous and dastardly Evil-in herself, a candle to light her way, and by her side, the sabre-tooth. His chest sank. The old lady was concentrating on keeping the candle upright. Gigi tugged at the hem of her dressing gown, the old lady looked down, her brow tightened. A large bony hand gripped a small boy's shoulder, *Got you!* A grip as firm as a car crusher claw.

Young Charles soon found himself accused of various criminal activities: breaking and entering, criminal damage, trespassing, menacing the elderly, and frightening a prize-winning pet. *Prize-winning!* said Charles. The parents took it all in good heart on Ms Dawn's behalf, for should she really be taken seriously? And Charles... wasn't he just an adventurous little boy? Ultimately, his marvellous sketches and insightful observations were sufficient to gain his parents' exoneration, and Charles went unpunished. Not surprisingly, this resulted in a local feud from which none of the parties ever really recovered, except perhaps for the young miscreant himself.

Evelyn Dawn continued to bill Hermione and Henrik for damage to the window frame until, some long months later, Henrik finally relented and paid up. The requested, then demanded, apologies, were never made.

Things ultimately faired worst for the cat, who was soon usurped by a Dobermann. Affectionately named Terror, his sole purpose: "To tear the flesh of trespassers, *especially the small ones!*"

In his own estimation, Charles felt this had been a thoroughly successful mission; one that had entailed unexpected challenges that he had risen to admirably, and overcome; added to which, he now had a pocketbook full of tales, diagrams and architectural reasoning, of which he was supremely proud.

Had Selené been there… if only Selené had been there, she would have marched young Arles to the folly herself, had him apologise and made to do useful chores for Ms Evelyn Dawn for quite some time as both reasonable and necessary recompense. But Selené was away in France, in Arles, her favourite place. The place after which she had romantically nicknamed her protégé, "A ferocious talent, and a will in need of guidance – what am I to do with you, little Arles!" Selené was the only person to get away with calling the proud Charles, 'little', in fact, he rather liked it, and he loved his special place in her affection, as though he was already aware of how rare and how truly valuable that would always be.

Chapter Twelve
Good Times

Gaia managed to slither into the bathtub and under the model opera house without disturbing it. She thought over the last of the letters. Selené was deeply disappointed in her, and acknowledging this set her ill at ease. She spilled the shivery waters over her body, and the body felt heavy, as though it might anchor below the tideline in shame. She lay in the shadow of the opera house, pondering different lines, thinking over a possible reply. She began to feel awkward about how she'd portrayed her relationship with Charles. Different blocks of memory shifted in and out of frame. She remembered how much she had adored Charles when they first met, how enchanting he was, how attractive his passion for architecture, how compelling it was simply to be in his company. All this was distant now, but so it had been, at first. Warm tears. She looked into the bleak white design of the opera house. – Swimming through the history of their marriage, perhaps it was finally time to remember more of the good times she had known with Charles, and perhaps some of these memories should now be shared with Selené.

Letter: I did love him

Gaia to Selené

Dear Selené,

Naïve, you call me naïve. You are right. You certainly have a penchant for straight talking. I rather envy that. I can hardly believe the things I think, the things I say, the things I get so wrong. This must have irritated Charles at times. It must have done. Don't worry, I am not about to wrap myself in self-pity.

I suppose that what I am trying to say, is that I'm sorry. I don't think I have managed to upset anyone quite as much as I have upset you. I think of what I have written to you, how stupid, moronic even... condescending... If I had a gun I ought to turn it on myself. But I would not have the courage. You, Selené, you have all the courage in the world. It's strange, but had it not been for Charles' death, I might never have known you, never shared in your thoughts, musings, or been subject to your great scoldings. How strange life is.

I also realise that since misreading his relationship with you, I have begun to condemn poor Charles completely in my own mind. What's wrong with me? Even when I discovered that he had not been living the kind of double life I had imagined, and that you were not his secret lover, I still pursued wrong thoughts about him. I still held him in darkness, I still wanted him to be wrong. There are acceptable wrongs — we're all of us flawed — but I wanted to bedevil my memory of him. What sinister woman am I?

Charles, yes, he was an egotist, yes he was selfish, obsessive, thoughtless, but he was many other things. Many other, many wonderful things.

When we first met, I was so smitten, thrilled even just to be near him. Power is very seductive, self-belief is captivating, I adored him. I adore him still.

We were in Berlin one time, he wanted to see one of Ralph Coover's buildings while it was still under construction, "More Americans building

89

in Berlin! Let's take a look!" he was quite put out. He wanted us to break into the site to take a look. He could have asked permission, and I'm sure he would have been granted access, but Charles was far too proud, and rather envious of Coover. He seemed to thrive on a sense of competition in the most boyish way, and at first even that held some allure. We sneaked into the site at night, forcing apart the corrugated iron that kept it hidden. He cut his arm getting in but it didn't put him off, he needed so many stitches later, it was a kind of madness. Once inside we ran about anarchically. I was never adventurous, not even as a child – I have never even so much as stolen an apple. And there we were, breaking in somewhere, it seemed so bad. So indescribably, intoxicatingly, bad. Uncharted ground. I thought we were like Bonnie and Clyde. So full of adrenalin I was buzzing with passion. I thought we would stop, kiss, tear away at each other's clothes, make love in the darkness, warm skin… sharp cool concrete – but no, not Charles…

Gaia stopped writing, her tears heavy with pain. She had no check on the words as they came, they flowed of their own volition. She took the pen and pierced the skin on the palm of her hand, and deeply. A moment passed, she acknowledged the stabbing pain, then clenched her fist around the bleeding, and went on writing –

…but I realise that when Charles was on an *Architectural Mission,* it was strictly that, and nothing but nothing must shake him from his cause. I didn't mind. I understood. And I knew that he liked the edge that denial and restraint gave him. And it was fun, we were like spies… silly and childlike, but it was wild wild fun.

Look at me, what am I writing? I will drive you insane with all of this! But I still can't help but feel such deep and hounding sadness.

I am glad to know you. I am glad to have known Charles.

Dear Selené, what must you think of me?

My love

Gaia

Letter: Nonsense

Selené to Gaia

Dear Gaia,

Firstly, and I quote:

If I had a gun I ought to turn it on myself. But I would not have the courage. You, Selené, you have all the courage in the world.

Do you recommend I shoot myself? I feel compelled, no matter how silly it looks, to write *ho ho ho!*, that you realise I do but jest, sweet Gaia, you quite entertain me!

Madam, you are now guilty of what you so often accuse me! Ignoring what I say and ask. So have you taken the postman to bed, or better still the Italian? I know for certain the latter to be something of a looker.

Darling, what can I say? Humdrum. Sexual humdrum. Charles, he peaked at many things in his life, but not, it is evident, in the bedroom, nor on the building site! Forgive my irreverence, my age allows it. You surprised me, there's hope for you, it seems you are at least adventurous of thought…

buzzing with passion, you say!

Oh, poor boy. Poor you! Sweet young Gaia, Charles, as you so rightly say, was many things, good and bad, but at most things, his score was brilliance. Now then, you shift from extremes, girl. Now that you have settled that he was not wicked, don't fool yourself that he was saintly, he was not. Don't kid yourself that there is anything truly laudable in his… what did you call it? Ah yes, *restraint,* for how can a woman feel appreciated around great *restraint,* as I see it implies here total abstinence and not merely… politeness… argh! That's not admirable child, that's abhorrent behaviour, and I would have told him as much.

wild wild fun, you say!

Well you can't fool me, *double* wild to describe the excitement of breaking into a building site with your lover, and *not* making passionate love therein! Sweet girl, *please!*

Sex, my dear, haven't I told you as much already? Sex is the most underestimated medicine, the most desperately torturesome pleasure, the most intoxicating, invigorating, mind-emptying bliss! Need I use yet still more words? It is many things. I do believe you know this, in theory at least, and I also believe you are desirous of all this being realised and more.

No, forget the postman. Go to Italy!

All the warmth of my heart

Selené

Letter: In Confusion

Gaia to Selené

Dear Selené,

I realise that much of what you say is meant as humour, but Charles... was my love. Why then do you encourage me to take another man to bed? Why do you want me so quickly to betray my Charles? I don't really believe you would mock me, but – *I don't understand!*

Yours

Gaia

Letter: To One in Distress

Selené to Gaia

Dear Gaia,

Look darling, it matters not a jot to me whether you take 'ten' men, or none to your bed. You see my directions as frivolous. Calm down dear, calm down. There is nothing frivolous about recovery, and by whatever means are possible and might help, you *will* recover yourself well enough, well enough to live and want to live. Now whether that means a man, as companion, as lover, or no, is of no matter. Perhaps it will be a house that makes the difference! I can't imagine you knocking about in that big old chunk of concrete by yourself, heavens. I remember the plans, bloody awful, I told Charles as much, he said it would 'do quite well', but dear, don't tell me that place suits you, I shall not believe you if you say as much. Only a similarly obsessive architect would be taken by such a place.

It may be a combination of things that aids your recovery, but what those components are is quite irrelevant. Build your own house! Take a lover! Take up gardening! But do something. Move life in some way, make shape, make waves, shake it a little. Without that, the rest of us are also dead.

There is something I have sensed about you all along Gaia, not only through our correspondence but also in Charles' and mine over the years. A sense that you are somehow afraid of life, wanting, yes, desirous, which is all well and good, but darling, at some point in this whole adventure, won't you allow yourself, to live? Will you live all your life as your shadow? Have you ever thought of taking part in your own life, come on, so far you have just been a passenger.

You have been too long asleep.

Darling, take up the challenge!

My love to you

Selené

Chapter Thirteen
Bigger and Better!

The last of the four architects that Gaia would include in the competition to design her home was none other than the American, Ralph Coover, peer and former roommate of the Italian, Alessandro.

Back in the Day…

American student-architect, Ralph Coover, was an unshaven brute, a lady-killer – or so he liked to think – but here's the thing, that *wifebeater* vest said something on the breast of a perfectly toned torso, that it really *did not* say on Ralph's not inconsiderable paunch. "Ralphi!" Alessandro would say – no one else would get away with calling Ralph Coover, *Ralphi,* but this was a liberty Ralph permitted his roommate, and later it came to represent their enduring friendship in a ferociously competitive architectural world – "Ralphi, what you have cannot be hidden, nor can it be overlooked, not by women of taste. You have to get that belly off you, and that is only the start of it. You don't reel in great women with fatty, flabby bait!" Ralph had to admit that the too-honest Italian probably had a point. Based on Alessandro's infallible talent on the dating front, and Ralph's serial *zero-ing*, Ralph soon conceded there was much his American butt and gut had to learn; and what a fortune cookie… the *I-talian Stall-ion* as tutor, way to go boy! – Coover's clichés drove Alessandro nuts, but what to do? "I sure struck lucky when I met you Ale-Zandro, so *row row row me boy,* out into the middle of that lake of seduction, and bap-tise me good!"

Alessandro Cannizzaro and Ralph Coover went way back. They shared their greenhorn architectural study days together in the States; each with the fire and desire of ten men; each out to mark his territory with the most dazzling architectural verve.

Ralph would spend his entire life with mismanaged romance, his greatest pastime outside of fishing. Could the two things be linked? Alessandro was never quite sure if fishing held any clues to Ralph's failed romantic life, but too close a relationship with flies and maggot-type-things surely wasn't attractive to anybody.

In terms of architecture, Ralph would stun the world. As a student, anything taught was negotiated and put to use, but when it came to practice… out in the real world, well, that was a totally different ball game. Ralph was to achieve a level of power never before granted an architect. The man had a fearlessness and a will so compelling that things simply fell in line with his dictate, BIG THINGS!

"He just gets his own bloody way! He assumes authority, almost *consumes* authority, always has done, seems to me… formidable swine! – Have to admire the bugger really. Has them all eating out of his hands, pretty much builds as he pleases; they fall over backwards for him! Big brute that he is. – All that power at his fingertips… thank Christ he isn't in politics! – I tell you, *not* being a politician, that's possibly Ralph Coover's only saving grace." These were the absentminded words of English architect, Edwin Ray, and naturally the ambitious young journalist, Ernest Wrightsin, was there to record them, printing them up later, under:

Architects – The Ultimate Megalomaniacs

It was a title that crossed the Atlantic, but Ralph only ever gave journalism a cursory glance, and his response, "Can you believe the shit they print over there? I'd say old Mr Ray there needs to calm down a little, give up the vino and take a man's drink, hell that's it! I'm gonna send him a case of bourbon," he grinned, generously; he knew the press took liberties.

During his career, Ralph Coover would gain 'The Power and The Glory', something he indulged himself in thoroughly in exchange for exercising his considerable architectural talents, and *that* he did like fish to water, *just swimmingly*. "My mother once told me I couldn't use architecture just to extend my childhood, stamping my feet to get my own way! I told her she was right, always was, and no way was this about childhood tantrums, not at all, *it was way bigger than that!*" He belly-laughed, "Way bigger, way bolder; and I remember giving her a big old squeeze as I told her, I wasn't playing like I was still a kid, no way. *I was playing God!* My poor mother looked so stunned when I said it, didn't know whether I was joking with her. And maybe I wasn't, difficult to know. Gave her a big kiss and another squeeze anyway. Heck, a boy's gotta have some fun. Take it to the edge."

Coover had a kind of grubby charisma, "Couldn't invent it if you tried," his grandfather would say. And as the ventures grew, so did Coover's confidence.

The endless explosion of skyscrapers cutting up the cityscape meant that in any cluster of closely built structures a building often found its double in the glass skin of another, and Coover had always been particularly struck if not often downright irritated by what he considered the ugliness of one building (if it wasn't his own) reflected in another – a kind of relationship that was struck up without invitation; an unwanted imprint that had no right being there. And Coover decided that as far as his structures were concerned, something was going to have to be done about this.

"Hell," he exclaimed, "I just put it to them, told it to 'em plain as I could, and nothing could have surprised me more when they just up and did what I asked 'em. ...'course it involved governors and all. That was the first time, after that they suckered along pretty well, and blow me now if they don't jump just as soon as I start up! Nowadays they mainly clear the surrounding site of what I call *unfit context*, way in advance." Unfit context, was Ralph's euphemism for:

Any other structure, be it permanent or transient, and most definitely including bill boards, sign boards and company logos – in any form, as these will not be permitted within a given radius to the Coover Work, without the prior consent of the Architect himself.

"Heck, if the suckers chew on it, what can I say?" It might not have seemed much on first hearing, but over time it lead in fact, to the razing to the ground of some monumental structures: office blocks, malls, you name it, if it *interfered* with *the necessary landscape for Coover Architecture*, if there was even the vague possibility that a company's

97

logo would be reflected in Coover's glass cladding – so giving them free advertising at certain sunny times of day – then it had to go, and not just the logo, but often the whole offending structure, in one instance: a thirty-storey office block. "I don't want dumb architecture reflecting its ass in *Coover Architecture*, simple as that." Of course, it was all tongue-in-cheek at the start, "But hell, Alessandro... *can you believe these suckers?* I'm cruising, riding these jerks like a herd of old donkeys, so who can blame me? And in the words of that great disco classic: *Ain't no stopping me now! I'm on the move!* – Whoop! Whoop!

Needless to say, Las Vegas was Ralph's least favourite place, "I hate all that junk that passes for architecture out there, ain't no thought... just a super over-build is all. Cheek by jowl junk. And most of all I hate the *trillion room hotels* and all the *loony-tune-replica-crap* they just keep on trawling out. For Christ's sake if people want *Venice*, go get the real thing! Hell, take a trip there! Venice, you chumps... is in Italy! Assholes! And by that I mean both the architects that build that crap *and* the folk that like it. I tell you, world's full of 'em."

Back in their study days, Ralph's sexual failings lay smouldering between the sheets shouting *unconsummated, untalented, zerooooooooo!*, but he never gave up completely. He'd read all the books, been to those ladies that train you up good, and so, thought Ralph, what gives? Still no luck. Truth of it was, Ralph never really got off the starting blocks. Daily bathing and deodorant might have helped; a good bicarb-toothpaste and a little nasal hair trim might have closed the gap some, but, as Alessandro none too gently pronounced, "There's a lot of work to do, Ralphi! A lot of catching up."

Weeks of late night conversations on the veritable art of dating were met by arguably poor results when the apprentice *Put it on the stage!* as Ralph was apt to describe it. Disheartened, Alessandro finally had to admit to being out of ideas, and he suggested Ralph take time out to consider for himself what might be going wrong. If Ralph couldn't see that 1960s flares, particularly worn that tight, might be part of what was scaring those girls away, then what was there to say? "But I likes 'em!" Ralph would chuckle while Alessandro shook his head.

Meanwhile, back on campus, the architectural design classes and the wildly animated discussion of crazy innovations, exposure to the extraordinary new uses of familiar materials coupled with the discovery of tantalising new ones, was nothing short of ecstasy. Taught only by the brilliant and borderline insane, challenging topics such as *legitimacy and design action and their interface with cultural boundaries* were also proving to be major hits. These two guys were wired with excitement, especially when set free in the Climate Chamber and the Lighting Lab where they regularly ran amok. They were having what Ralph readily christened, "*One inte-llectual orgasm after another!* It's a rollercoaster ride is what it is Alessandro, and it's ours for the taking!"

The future lay before them in smart concrete set in stunning free-form configurations, super-strength structural-glazing, and eco-friendly tree-free hardwoods – and the world of architecture…? Well that could only lay prostrate before the brilliance of their as yet only imagined, almost unthinkable, sometimes nigh on unbuildable designs. OK, they weren't there yet, "But," said Ralph, "we're about to a-*rrive!*" And to the delight of them both, he wasn't wrong.

Semesters came and went, and whilst visiting family back home for the holidays, Alessandro truly hoped that Ralph had either made a genuine leap, *critical mass and all*, in the love laboratory, or had at least found a hobby to replace his interest in love. Something, aside from fishing (though he didn't mind the odd trip himself now and again).

When the young Italian returned to the States to face a shiny new semester, he did so with a spring in his step. He'd missed his American buddy, and everything else aside, they were getting to share some of their most important years together, including nurturing a mutual and unparalleled passion for architecture.

As Alessandro strolled back up the street he thought he could hear music coming from some place. A few steps closer and a horrible wailing was added to what was otherwise a classic Motown track. It was a new year; a new, two-man shared apartment, but Alessandro was already seriously doubting that Ralph had learnt any new tricks outside the architectural arena. And he was right, but you gotta admire a man for trying! Don't you? Ralph… was singing.

Cue the music!

'You are Everything' by Marvin Gaye:

Ooh, you are everything,
And everything is you,
Ooh ooh…
Ooh-ooh!

There are certain tracks that should carry laws, possibly, *arguably*, ALL tracks. That is, that once any individual has established, beyond any, but at least *reasonable* doubt, that he or she cannot sing a damn note, that they be forbidden to exercise their vocal equipment in that manner, EVER. That only seems decent, and anyone who was in the neighbourhood that day, sorely, SORELY, agreed.

Alessandro knew and liked the Marvin Gaye version, his mother had been a fan, but Ralph's rendition, well that was a concrete-shattering experience, without support, and in need of condemnation, termination, anything! Just make him stop! Alessandro pushed open the door in trepidation, "Hey my friend, so good to see you! *But really Ralphi, you so got to halt the singing, really, there's something truly undignified about singing that song like that… and in front of a mirror!* Please, you have skills for other things, it's too much to branch out that far. And you simply cannot sing! If it's about women, well Ralph, seriously, women don't see you how *you* see you, that's harsh of me, but I can't take any more if we are going to live together and study together this year. *I can't!*"

Ralph looked sulky, but only for two seconds, then he embraced his buddy, he'd really missed him. Ralph was clad in the thickest of skin, and he didn't quite get it, what was up with women anyhow? When he looked at his image in the mirror, he got: tenderness, a masculine jawline, someone kinda cute at the eyes, hell, they must be blind! And singing? Come on, who doesn't want to be serenaded?

The Grown-up Guys…

Now there are two things that the full-grown architect, when drunk, should steer clear of discussing. The first, no surprise, is architecture, the second, is sex. But when Ralph and Alessandro ever got together, reunions, weddings, fishing trips, these were the two things neither of them could hold back talking about.

Alessandro finished his cigarette and took up the next glass of bourbon, "There are some things to which a man is suited, if you are lucky you may be suited to more than one thing. Not you Ralphi, not you. You have something working well for you, you are a god in our world, almost despite yourself. You make bureaucrats, planners, and global monster corporations wrap themselves around your fingers, fall at your feet, to take it where it's not sunny…"

"Up the ass!"

"You didn't have to say it, *argh!* What can I do with you, Ralph? You really should stop that too-dirty talk, you are still not forty but all your life you are a dirt-brain, filthy-stinking… stinking man, when it comes down to it. Now, without you interrupting me anymore, just let me speak… OK, so you build your mad ideas, but then you make everyone rearrange the landscape around, to suit it! To suit your building! I never achieved that. No one, no one ever achieved that, not on this scale, not in so many ways, never!"

"That's right," said Ralph, "shit, I never thought I could pull it off, then I'd done it once, and the rest – listen to me, I sound like a movie star! – " then, mimicking the voice and swagger of John Wayne, "The rest, is, as they say, history!" They laughed together, and Alessandro carried on, "Yeah, I might never achieve that part, but you, you will never make a lover."

Coover sat down again, "OK, like I ain't heard you a zillion times! But you really expect me to stop tryin'? My pecker ain't getting any less in-er-ested even if the rest of me's facing a few facts, hell I even stopped fartin' in front of women! But I don't see why I should—if it's my home, me paying the hotel bill. Jee-sus, all that fuss to win a girl, and to think that all it takes is just a little *iddy-biddy* fart to ruin things! Even engineers ain't that easily upset."

Alessandro poured the dregs of the bottle between them, shaking his head all the while and grinning ear to ear, safe in the knowledge that he was still at least 'one' of the best architects in the world, and something of a lover, his friend would never be.

Chapter Fourteen
Alessandro Cannizzaro's Shoes

Ralph is in Italy for a brief visit. He sits, jetlagged and dumbstruck, in the presence of Alessandro. He's listening to his dear old buddy over a rather luscious dinner, but wanting it to be over so that they can hit the bourbon. Bourbon never helps Ralph's hangovers, insomnia or jetlag, but his firm belief that it will rarely wavers.

Alessandro is delivering his *Shoe Monologue*. Ralph is sure he's heard most of it before, but he never fails to be dazzled by the prowess of this *serious seducer*.

Like the mailman, Tom Bradshaw, Alessandro has a thing for Marilyn Monroe, not with quite the same need-to-cuddle gorgeous-bosomy-roundedness that Tom yields to, but in an equally appreciative, if slightly more sophisticated way. During his early twenties, Alessandro became quite philosophical about the art of seduction, and its practice and pursuance were treated with the reverence other guys reserved for soccer, chess or gambling.

One of Alessandro's proudest, though at first glance, none too impressive, conclusions, was that a man should be extremely careful in his choice of gifts, especially when in pursuit of that most special of women, *a Marilyn*. He told Ralph, "Never present a woman with lingerie," not because it is too personal or could be construed as one of self-interest, but simply because nothing compares with nakedness – certainly not at bedtime. That was the first consistency with Monroe's life – bedtime was bare-time. The second... was shoes, and Marilyn Monroe adored shoes... very particular shoes. Alessandro avidly studied video footage, books, movies, and old newspaper clippings, anything he could lay his hands on, trying to glean as much as he possibly could about how Marilyn felt about shoes. As wacky as it sounds, what Alessandro came to understand about *women and shoes* was an education most guys never got, but which most would trade some treasure for.

"Ralphi, let me tell you something truly special. My greatest romantic secret. Shoes! And Ralphi, not just any shoes, only the best shoes in the world, *Salvatore Ferragamo*, Italian – of course." Ralph rolled his eyes, and wondered why Italians ate such darn small portions, luckily he wasn't too hungry, but for breakfast he might have to order double. A big brain needs a big feed! You don't get to be Ralph Coover by being underfed… he suddenly realised he'd stopped paying attention.

"Listen to me, Ralph. You see, the French may think it sexy to spray their women; the Belgians to make them fat with chocolate; Germans, to make them fatter still with cake and sausage; the English, well what can I say, I think they do nothing; The Japanese paint them so thickly… like oil on canvas, how can I kiss that? But the Italian spirit shows that to know a woman is to adore her, and to adore her from the feet upwards. From the tips of her toes. – Most women, of course, don't *look* like Marilyn, but let me tell you, every woman wants to feel like her. That's the secret. – As I say, most don't look like her – but I never cared only for blondes – and it's not about colouring, it's about *essence*. I tell you, every country has its Marilyns, they might be dark-skinned or lightly sun-kissed; tall and skinny; medium brunette, but they have Marilyn about them, or, they should have. And the trick is – I learned this by twenty-two and after that, I just perfected it – you treat her like Marilyn, and you got her! For the most special ones that means shoes. Salvatore Ferragamo! The reason? That was Marilyn's favourite shoe designer – I can't say *cobbler*, what kind of word is that to be used for the glove of the foot? I found this word next to *shoemaker* in my English dictionary, it was quite horrible. *Cobbler!* No.

"So, Ferragamo realised that the height of shoe Marilyn found most comfortable was approximately four inches, that's quite a few centimetres – the point is, that she wanted a specific height. Four inches was ideal, and so for her they specialised in this height. Wonderful! I visited many shoe shops and realised that for a woman, to have the most beautiful shoes is a very sensual, almost erotic experience, especially if they are of the highest quality, superb design, and ridiculously expensive. Ferragamo fits the bill perfectly. Allow a woman to be as magnificent as she ought to be, and you may discover a woman who becomes even more magnificent!"

Ralph suppressed a belch, and in doing so felt a small moment of pride, he rubbed his belly, "That was great, shall we order some bourbon now?" Alessandro ignored him and carried on.

"In my life, I never asked another man's advice about women, never! Yes my father taught me a few things, but most I learned from him was in watching, observing... and most of the time he did a poor job at seducing my mother. He was a busy man, but *I*... I am also a busy man!

"Ralphi, what I learned, I learned from women themselves, from looking, from their psychology, from what raises a smile. Mostly it's simple. Women, they are just people most of them, and some of them are more, and a few are outstanding, and more so when you love them. Flowers only bloom fully for those who know how to handle them, and in my case, my sense for nature lies at the 'feet' of beauty. Think about it, Marlene Dietrich, Katherine Hepburn, Greta Garbo, and of course... Marilyn, they all wore Ferragamo. For sure they must have worn other designers too, but come on, I'm Italian! And so, it's the Florentine Ferragamo," Alessandro sighed, contented. "Florence... that's where he settled... you see his good taste!"

Ralph smiled but by now he really needed that drink, he wiggled the stem of his empty glass somewhat forlornly, and finally! Finally, Alessandro took the hint, "OK... but, no dessert?"

"Nope!" Jetlag and too much ear-bashing were clearly taking their toll, Ralph NEVER refused dessert. Alessandro was too preoccupied with his own stories to act on his surprise, "No dessert. That's fine, but some bourbon for sure. Let me get the waiter."

"Good idea, my friend. – Wow, that dinner was *divine,* d'ya get it, Zandro? *Deee-vine!*" Ralph chuckled to himself. He had almost passed out when he first became aware – back in the day – that Alessandro was bedding one of their professors, Simone Divine, *Miss De-vine.* So many years had passed but it was still a real vicarious pleasure to revisit Alessandro's 'love past' – it was also cringingly fun to bring up the more embarrassing encounters. Ralph himself had never caught up on the love front, such a phenomenal latecomer in fact that he had eventually tried to argue that he was intentionally holding back, in order to derive something more useful from this sexual tension… redirecting the energy – much in the way Charles Ore would have prescribed –*to enhance creative potential*, but that never washed with Alessandro. That said, Ralph could hardly be blamed for making up cover stories, in their first year of sharing, he was kicked out of that dorm room far more often than was reasonable; and not wanting this issue to come between them, Ralph had ultimately put the Italian's phenomenal promiscuity down to loneliness… him being so far away from home and all. But Alessandro wasn't homesick, and Ralph… Ralph wasn't saving himself.

Ralph sensed his host wasn't quite done with droning on and asked that they be brought a full bottle of bourbon and that it be left at the table. He poured the first glass, knocked it back like a miracle cure, and poured some more. Then he started in on the most hilarious imitation of Alessandro, and loud, *"Never take a woman too seriously – that I learned from my father,* wow I was blown away by all that stuff when I first met you, and look at you! Still the same old panache, *Zandro.* Too suave for me. You're one on your own and that's for sure. But hey, you left out Americans in your *who's the best lover* list, so how do we guys figure in the seduction stakes?"

"Americans, well what can I say, I never saw you in action, Ralph – so what is there to say?"

"You're such a tease," but Ralph was understandably somewhat hurt by this remark.

"You know Ralph, I used to love American girls, but now they cut themselves up like turkeys, sewing the parts back together tight, adding bits in, injecting stuff… I don't get it, must be so painful, and in the end it isn't pretty." He finished on the poorest possible imitation of Ralph, *"No man, I like my women real!"*

"Shit! Was that supposed to be *me?*" Ralph laughed now and raucously, "Give it up, dude! Hell, it's really great to see you, you got better lookin' if that was ever possible, but other than that I have to say, you ain't changed a bit! – Can't say the same for your design, man, that's shooting right off the scale. I can't believe what you're starting to get away with. Still, I guess hanging around with me was bound to

106

rub off somehow, and I ain't heard you fart once yet!" he chuckled on, "Impressive Alessandro, yup that's the word for it, darn impressive."

It would come as no surprise to either of these architects to find themselves part of the very select number invited to compete and design for Charles Ore's widow. – Gaia Ore, having previously forgone a place that felt like home, would now come to settle for nothing less. She would choose only those architects who, despite their involvement in grand scale endeavours, had proved both in the essays they published and in their builds, that they understood most thoroughly the requirements for a quality of living: the experience of the dweller; that the outside must matter as much as the inside, and that for something to be called home, be it simple or exquisite, lay the prerequisite desire and intention for the balance of aesthetics and tranquillity with utility and rationality. – Ralph, more than any of them hated pretention, and this last part he described as "gotta be comfortable, gotta like it."

Over the years Alessandro's boldness had bolted the stable. These days, he was out there, running headlong and free, and nothing, *but nothing*, could hold him back. Perhaps he *had* learned a thing or two from Ralph Coover, but however it might be explained, it was a level of confidence that was now way off the sonar. When someone gets it so right, though their ideas seem unfathomable but the drive to prove them whips your feet from under you and shoots you way on up with the buzz of cocaine just from sniffing in the clearest, cleanest air, well what are you going to do? Soon, no one could deny him.

Competitions lined themselves up. There were the usual kinds of restriction in most of the briefs, but the one that irritated Alessandro most was always the *given* location. The way Alessandro saw it, most clients got this part wrong, they got other things wrong too – like the budgets, *Hey, are they crazy!* But where they went most wrong was in deciding the site for the new design. Alessandro would rather bow out of a major competition than compromise his belief that *The Architect* was the one best qualified to choose the setting for his architecture. So whilst Ralph had other architecture floored to create his *ideal context,* the Italian regularly informed his clients that they had chosen the wrong site and had best follow *his* advice on where to set *his* architecture. In the case of a grand naval museum in the US, he argued ferociously that the best place for it was *not* next to the *Mad-Axe Multiplex Cinema, Fun Plaza* and *Freddy's Friendly Family Diner!* No. Absolutely not. Alessandro Cannizzaro knew the perfect site, and Alessandro Cannizzaro demanded the perfect site. – The museum should be set close to the beach, with the gentle movement of the tide as background, the scenery changing in gradual shades of turquoise, white and grey; the sounds and moods of the sea providing the ideal 'aural context'; and with the smell and taste of salt in the air to sharpen the senses. *This* was how the public would best be prepared to appreciate the museum and its exhibits! This was how it should be! He waited whilst the powerful deliberated, praying his bluff would not be called.

The museum... was built by the beach.

He reflected that perhaps all architects need the good fortune of being born to an indulgent Italian mother. He looked again at her photograph, and kissed her.

This powerful but mutable client – and so early on in Alessandro's career – had generously, and unwittingly, made a rod for the backs of all Alessandro's future clients. *Bravo!* He had lift off! From then on it was full-blown architectural thrills and spills all the way, beautifully wild, and just about as far from architectural plain sailing as he could get. Just as he desired. *Oh Mama!*

Back in the UK, Edwin Ray's latest design proposals were attracting very little interest. He felt he was losing his edge. He felt buried by the Coover and Cannizzaro mavericks and their *novelty architecture!* He had much admired Charles Ore. Somehow he felt he knew what he was up against with Charles, a tough contender, yes, but not out of his league, and the two big 'Cs' seemed to be jacking up the heat to an unbearable level. Since embarking on *realised architectural projects*, Edwin suffered terribly when his designs were rejected and he often wished he had been content to bask in the glory of his *theoretical* success. Of all the architects, Edwin Ray would be especially pleased to receive an invitation to submit a design for Charles Ore's widow, for that way, he was still a contender!

Ralph coughed a little as Alessandro lit a cigarette, "Zandro, did you read about Charles Ore kicking the bucket? I almost died myself when I read it – died laughing that is, 'course I know I shouldn't, but shit! How the hell'd he manage to go and die on a piece of fish for heaven's sake? Eel wasn't it?"

"Yes, I believe so. That was really awful."

"Awful *funny!*"

The too men drank down their bourbon and shared a quiet moment – on the verge of respect. "D'ya go the funeral? I thought as maybe you knew him? I read he studied in the US, but never crossed paths with him myself. From what I heard, the guy always struck me as something of an asshole…"

"No, I nearly met him, a few times, but no, I wasn't at the funeral."

"His wife's a looker, you see her alongside him in one of the magazines? 'Course they all did darn long articles on him after he'd gone."

"Yes, she looks very attractive," Alessandro exhaled and examined his cigarette, "You know, I would really like to meet her."

"Hey! What kind of an ass are you? Jumping his Mrs before he's even cold!"

"No!…"

"Gotcha!" Ralph chortled, "Hey, just kiddin' around Zandro! Take it easy. I couldn't give two hoots about old Ore, the guy's been dead ages now anyhow. You get yourself in there, tickle her toes an' all. Maybe even buy her some of them fancy shoes you're always on about!" He chuckled warmly now, downing another bourbon.

After Ralph had left, Alessandro wondered if enough time had elapsed to permit another letter to the widow. And it didn't take him long before he decided that yes, time enough had passed.

Letter: From the Italian

Alessandro Cannizzaro to Gaia

Dear Mrs Ore,

I should like to call you Gaia, if you would permit. Somehow, I feel I know you, I don't know why, but I sense in you something of a kindred spirit. I do not worry that you will find my words too bold, for I believe you will appreciate them as honest. Your last correspondence was most kind, you have a generous nature.

I think that a change of atmosphere, of air, of company, can all be quite therapeutic, and it is in this belief that I should like to invite you again to my country. I think you are very polite and would not accept on first invitation, and so I make it again, and hope that time enough has passed for you to feel able to accept and take a small journey. Italy waits for you.

Yours

Alessandro

Alessandro immediately began to fantasise that she might accept:

First, you have to have a brilliant idea,
When you got the brilliant idea —
Then you start to make believe it's true,
And once you can see it as a full picture,
A reality,
Then, you as good as have it!

Alessandro had no problem implementing this theory of success, it had certainly worked with his architecture. He mailed the letter, confident in the belief that this time, she would indeed accept.

Chapter Fifteen
Plans

Gaia now made a study of Selené's letters. She began to copy them out in parts, paragraphs, sentences, single words, paring down as she went:

Build your own house! Take a lover! Take up gardening! But do something. Move life in some way, make shape, make waves, shake it a little. Without that, the rest of us are also dead.

Go to Italy!

Will you live all your life as your shadow? Have you ever thought of taking part in your own life, come on, so far you have just been a passenger.

You have been too long asleep.

Darling, take up the challenge!"

Another cigarette, a drop more whiskey, then she scribbled over some parts, blocking them out, refining the list. Fine-tuning.

These days she only slept in her study. She had long since accepted Charles' room as a 'purely' *creative unit*, and it had never really been a room for lovers, never really their bed-room. She didn't even like to go in anymore. She sat in her study at the desk in the rosy-jamas, hiking socks and an old cardigan. Halfway through a pack. The list was now quite modest:

house
lover
gardening
Italy
passenger

She scrutinised the words, wondering, questioning. She would deal with each in turn starting from the bottom of the list. She drew a line under *passenger*, Selené was right, she had always been a passenger in her life. She had never taken control or responsibility. She had taken the easy route, followed someone who was driven; luxuriated in their success and its rewards; never taken risks of her own design. She began to appreciate that reflected glory was only that, nothing more than a shadow of feeling.

Italy, she put a question mark by its side, she'd always wanted to go; now she had an invitation, a repeated invitation – Mr Cannizzaro seemed curious and kind – she looked down at her pyjamas and smiled, amused. Perhaps.

Gardening, no, that wasn't going to be part of the plan. She struck a line through it straight away. *Gardening...* no, that felt *too* challenging.

Lover, she glanced down again at *Italy*, and perplexed, left it as it was.

House, house she thought, home, Charles what did you build? She had wondered previously about the 'new house plans' he had evidently shown Selené, but for some reason she had never wanted to see them. Never thought to ask Selené for details, or where they might be. And neither would she. She couldn't have answered why, she simply felt... disinclined. There were moments when she felt she *ought* to try to find them, and more than that, perhaps even have them followed through – other widows would! She stopped herself and exhaled. *Ought to!* What rubbish! *Passenger!* She felt she could hear Selené's voice, as though she would know it without ever having heard it, *Passenger!*

Passengers, she concluded, are those who: *ought to, ought to do this, ought to do that,* but since she was no longer going to be a passenger, then from all associated obligations, she was absolved; *but other widows, and what they would do?* Other widows be damned. She scribbled out *passenger* aggressively. Now she was left with a remarkably short list:

house
lover
Italy

She put down the pen, pleased. She rolled her shoulders in satisfaction, poured another whiskey, and lit up afresh.

Letter: Onwards and Upwards

Gaia to Selené

Dear Selené,

Alright, finally I got it! *Je comprend!* You are right about so many things, I almost hate you for it! And this time, trust, that for once, I am jesting.

I feel a sudden rush of soberness, of clarity. It feels, marvellous. I hold your letters very close to my heart. It is time to make a few decisions!

One thing I have in mind, is indeed to find a house, or have one built, one that will be my home. I have never felt at home here, I love certain things about the Construct, but am not, nor have ever been, able to relax sufficiently to call it 'home'. I am not, however, entirely sure how to go about discovering this 'place' that will be home, but perhaps that is just a matter of time, and gradually I will work it out. I have made myself a list of things to help *move* my weakened state towards something of a recovery, but I have no idea how the various things might be accomplished, if indeed they are possible at all, still, I must try. I am more awake than I have been for months, and that is at least, and *at last*, something of a start.

My love to you

Gaia

Letter: DIY

Selené to Gaia

Dear Gaia,

Now then, I will get round to discussing your plans, a house and so forth, but before I forget, I must tell you that, finally, I have bothered to look out a few photographs to send you, and I will endeavour to write the dogs' names on there somewhere, they might amuse. I am a terror for promising things and not delivering.

I recently took on a young man, although hardly *that* young in the scheme of things, I should say he's close to fifty-five. Anyway, I took him on, on the pretext of helping me out with the more tiresome aspect of gardening, namely – digging. But naturally, I'm perfectly capable of that myself. Healthy longevity, I tell you darling, if only I could bottle it! I'd make a veritable fortune. Anyway, that's by the by. The pretext, yes… well I had to invent something as I took rather a shine to him, he's a horseman, a retired racehorse owner, entrepreneur or so… self-made type of chap. I dare say many of those terms are redundant these days, unfashionable; is it still appropriate to describe a person as 'self-made' nowadays? I wonder if it hasn't been usurped by some other term; and people, in general, make so little of themselves and of their lives anymore, perhaps there's no need of it at all. Well anyway, this chappy, 'horseman' I have chosen to call him, he has wonderful good strong legs, and has become my lover of late. Quite a one he is. I must not allow him to form any unacceptable attachment, I can't abide those who cling, but I'm sure he'll be sensible.

Now then, the 'home' plans, why not design it yourself? You can't possibly have spent all that time with Arles, and not picked up a thing or two. In any case, if need be, you could have someone else check over the designs as you go along. Yes, build it yourself, why not?!

Dear girl, I must sign off now, they're barking!

Love to you

Selené

Letter: Photographs

Gaia to Selené

Dear Selené,

Selené you are so vital, so full of life, and I, still so far from living. As you once pointed out, it may well be something that has been true of me all along, perhaps for my whole life. I have been dead whilst living. I know you will deny it, but you are an inspiration. I'm so lucky that our paths have crossed.

You and the *horseman!* Goodness, you'll laugh at me, but I was surprised despite all your 'waking me, and shaking me', it seems I have only thought of such scenes in novels or perhaps in film. How magical, that someone's real life is so infinitely beautiful, so shot through with passion. I am now just thirty-three, but have not half your courage, charisma nor spontaneity, would that I had. Perhaps there is still time.

I love the photographs you sent. The spaniels are gorgeous, and your names for them: *Great Catherine* – That's after Catherine the Great I suppose; *Lizzy 1st* – must be Queen Elizabeth I, and *Sulky 'bo*, is that after Garbo? Then, Avignon, Cimiez and Toulouse – places you are most fond of in France, like Arles! I love them! The names and the pictures! There was no picture of you, but I should have expected that now that I know you more, and somehow I have an idea of who you are and how you might appear without visual clues. I am blind, so to say, but not. I can well imagine you chasing after the spaniels and calling out their ridiculous names, so funny, so full of life. I can't help it, but I do still wish that we could meet.

Did you realise you sent one picture by accident? It was just a tiled floor! I suppose, like me, everyone takes a few odd shots whilst fumbling with their camera. Charles would always scold me for my lack of concentration.

In terms of the 'home plan', no, I cannot see me designing it, but I really think that a new place would make all the difference to me. I am toying with the idea of commissioning someone. What do you think?

My warmest wishes

Gaia

Letter: A Competition!

Selené to Gaia

Dear Gaia,

Well aren't you a one! Where from comes this new found confidence and dalliance with mockery? The spaniels' names are not ridiculous! And what of *you*, named 'Gaia' of all things, Greek mythology, I know a little, my own name taken from the same, but Lordy, your name means *Primeval Earth Goddess!* Heavens above, sweet girl! No wonder Charles took a fancy to you. I think you'll have to agree that even 'Catherine the Great' sounds tame next to that. *Selené*, if you've an interest, my own good name, means *moon goddess*, I think that sits well with one of my disposition, enjoying a solitary life and fond of the dark. Simple pleasures. And by the way, you were right, Sulky 'bo is Greta Garbo, you waken slowly, but now you do at least attempt to open your eyes.

The picture of the tiled floor darling, is a particularly important one, I am not clumsy with the camera. I am not clumsy at all, nor do I fumble! I had just cleaned the kitchen floor, something I do none too regularly, I do so hate cleaning, and it was all sparkling, no, *gleaming!* And I thought to myself, golly that is clean, I must just take a picture of it while it looks so beautiful. It's really not a good thing to clean too often, that way, when one does, it really shows. Yes, it looks all the better for the contrast. I do hope you are not one of the over-domesticated breed. Hateful.

You continue, in some measure, to insinuate that my years denote something ailing. You do so in expressions of far too much surprise with regard to my romantic conquests. Desist! Be impressed by all means, but 'surprised', no. *You*, may well be suffering a kind of accelerated decrepitude − which I sincerely hope we can reverse − but please do not attribute the same to me. I was born with an old head on my shoulders, but bloody well vow to die young!

Now then, the matter of the house. I have it! If you cannot see yourself designing it, why not run it as a competition? That way you can engage the skills of several leading architects, and choose from among a number of marvellous designs. I suggest between four and six as a good number to invite to such a competition, choose only from the best. I would recommend at least that you include the Italian, and I am myself rather taken by the work of that Spaniard – Carlos Santillana. You must have favourites of your own, these are but suggestions, but think how exciting it could be!

There now, I have rattled on, enough. The horseman calls!

My love to you

Selené

Chapter Sixteen
No Good!

Another day, another mailbag. Tom was missing Cara and the kids. They were staying over at her mother's as punishment for his *being no good*. Unaccustomed as he was to deception, Tom hadn't covered his tracks well at all, and Cara, her middle name *Suspicion* had discovered a receipt for pyjamas, ladies pyjamas, rose-pink pyjamas – oh yes, it said as much on the receipt – in Tom's jacket pocket. His friend had given him the receipt along with the parcel, and Tom's mistake… was to keep it. He'd used his friend's address, but his own name, *shit*, but it was too late, and now he had it coming to him. Full force. Cara had naturally wanted to know all kinds of things relating to these pyjamas, for a start, where were they? "You didn't buy 'em for me now did ya, 'cos I just had my birthday and all's I got was a bunch o' dopey old flowers, *Dopey-ass!* And I don't wear nothin' in bed, 'cos *you* don't like me to!" She was right about that, except that she'd have slept naked her whole life anyway. "*Soooo* Tom, who in hell's name you been buying gifts for? And where d'ya get the money?" That was a major sticking point, now he had to confess to lying about how much he'd won on the scratch card.

Cara, having smacked the *gui-tar* good and hard against the wall, then danced all over Tom's pride and joy. She did this, in her stilettos. And she sang:

Dance, dance, dance, on Do-pey-Tom's gui-tar!

Tom Jones would have been as disturbed by the battering of lyrics and their shrieked delivery, as Tom Bradshaw was by the total annihilation of his *other love*.

"Men ain't s'posed to cry tears this big, Cara. Not my gui-tar babe, not my gui-tar!" But she was having none of it, and he needed to *quit being one too-big-baby, or else!* It was a tough situation, but he stopped crying. She interrogated him into the early hours. Were the *girl-pyjamas* his? Was he a serious cross-dresser? Tom wasn't too sure what separated 'serious' cross-dressers from any other kind, but he didn't ask her to explain, he just carefully held his mailbag over his groin – in times gone by, he'd seen those stilettos fly. She went on. Was he having an affair? Who with? For how long? How could she believe even one word he said? The rest just all became a big old mangled mess in his tormented head. Cara went around and around and around, and nothing rang true. By four in the morning he was so exhausted he was tempted to invent an affair just to satisfy her, *just to shut the bitch up!* He didn't often want to call her names, but shit, she was going way overboard. Then he remembered, he *had* stolen the scratch card, he *had* lied, hidden things, *and* bought a gift for another woman, hell, Cara was right, he was bad!

The next morning, when they'd all upped and left, he was feeling out of sorts, and out of favour. Imagine how pleased he was when he finally got to work and discovered a letter from Italy as part of Mrs Ore's mail. Mail, from Alessandro Cannizzaro! That Alessandro, he was a genuine... a gen-u-ine nice guy. He remembered Alessandro's gentle turn of phrase, he remembered the invitation to Italy. He knew she hadn't gone, mailmen can tell when the occupants are away, and she hadn't been anywhere, and he speculated that it might be nice for her, change of scenery and all, that had to help. He didn't open this letter; although glad to have read the first one, a part of him knew it was pretty bad to keep on with that type of thing. Letters, they're private type-things. He grew sentimental; that morning he'd walked out of his own miserable front door and straight into a gloom-cloud. He missed his occasional morning banter with Charles. Charles' passing had put the natural rhythm of his deliveries out of step. His day had partly unravelled. For a posh, ed-jucated kind of guy, Charles was alright. Why was it always the good ones that died too soon? Tom felt forlorn, then he glanced back down at the mail, pleased that at least there seemed to be another good guy, despite his being Italian and all, that cared in some measure for the widow. He couldn't help himself, and despite the severe bullying that Mrs Ore had cost him, he still felt compassionate towards her, he still didn't like to think of her all alone in the world. A letter from a good guy in Italy, that was nice. The sun came out, hey, life goes on, he muttered to himself, smiling as he pushed Gaia's letters through the door.

As he wandered back up the street, he heard a dog barking, it made him wince. He thought about Perry, the baby they'd lost. He thought about the dog. He wished he'd never bought that stupid pit bull. He wished he'd never set eyes on Poochi, what the hell kind o' stupid name was that anyway? What was it with people, that they always gotta give pets such dumb-ass names? Stupid name, stupid dog! Stupid me! Tom was in the habit of blaming himself, and as Cara had pointed out at the funeral, buying that dog was all Tom's *stupid fault, stupid idea,* and he *was the dumbest excuse for a father a kid could ever have.* She had to be right, she always was, he sobbed under his cap, hiding from the glare of the sunshine. Sometimes I just hate the sun! Then he realised he was talking to himself and sobbed a little deeper into his handkerchief.

He'd thought the funeral would finish him off, it wasn't right to bury your child before yourself, specially not a little 'un. Little Perry, little coffin, little life. It was cold the day of the funeral, Tom felt his marrow like brittle ice running through his no good bones. Throughout his life, Tom had been given plenty of opportunity to feel no good, other people, usually women, helped him feel that way, but this day, he didn't need any help. This day things were plain and ice cold clear. He was no good. No good at all.

He hauled himself back into the present, Perry had been dead ages now, but it wasn't an easy thing to get over, and he probably never would. He realised he'd stopped delivering letters. His face was red with crying, and hell, there might even be more – he hated how tears could come up like that, out of nowhere, and take even the strongest of men by surprise. Shit! He couldn't face the possibility of bumping into anyone, not any of those people, behind those doors, or those crossing his path as they headed off to their asshole jobs, so he cut his round short, his mailbag still half full. WELL SO WHAT! They could wait another day, assholes! People in those fancy houses, middle class, upper-middle-class ponces, with their smug little lives, assholes mostly anyways, yeah, they could wait! His legs were almost jelly, he had to pull himself together.

He figured Cara hadn't really meant what she'd said about him being a useless father, a no-good husband. Women say that stuff when they're upset, it's normal, right? Had to be, his mum was the same way, and shit she'd had a lot to put up with, his dad being no good, and then him being a disappointing son. Hell, women, gotta give birth and all that stuff, seems like most of 'em never get over it. If they talk about the pain still, when you're a full grown man, then that has to be one big kind of pain, right? Tom found himself starting to laugh through the weight of his tears. My ma used to say I was *the dumbest excuse for a kid a mother could ever have,* and now my Cara says I'm *the dumbest excuse for a father a kid could ever have!* Ah shit, those women deserve better than that. He would just have to try harder.

He rounded another corner, gradually the tears slowed, and then dried up. He felt calmer, too calm, almost dead on his feet. He looked down at his mailbag.

Ah shucks! I ain't never missed my round, 'cept for funerals, and the time I was really sick, and I ain't gonna start now! Tom checked that his face was free of escaping tears. Then he delivered the rest of the mail.

Cara, she had a very particular kind of tongue, the same kind of tongue Tom's mother had, the kind that needed snipping.

Chapter Seventeen

Delusion

Gaia was surprised and pleased to receive another letter from *the Italian*. Another invitation, and more beautiful words. Alessandro had a charisma that lifted from the page, a gentleness, a warmth of spirit. Italy, Italy, Italy! Gaia managed to fool herself well enough that she had no real interest in meeting Alessandro himself, but that she simply must get away for awhile; would benefit from a change of scenery, a different air... a change of pace. So yes, she would visit Italy, and she would accept the architect's invitation. For if she was to include him in The Competition – *Selené, you have the most wonderful ideas* – then it would not do to be impolite, and it would seem ungracious not to accept. – The English, and those raised by them, often enjoy the luxury and convenience of self-deception; and Gaia, adopted by the same, was influenced by the blindest, bluest English blood.

Letter: *Yes, yes yes!*
Gaia to Selené

Dear Selené,

Forgive me, you must know by now, I mean you no offence, I just have these clumsy ways of expressing myself. I believe you and I could easily step into each others' age quite comfortably, I am certainly far closer to old in any pejorative sense, than you, and you quite clearly are bountifully blessed by youth.

How sweet and funny, that you record your freshly-cleaned floor!

Now then, I am desperate to tell you these things – firstly that I believe your idea of a competition is an absolute winner! Secondly, that I have heard from the Italian again, another invitation, and feel that I simply have to accept, particularly if I am going to ask him to submit a design, which is exactly what I have in mind. I would like to follow your advice and include Carlos Santillana, although I do have reservations about his work, I know he has an obsession with 'transience and immediate shelter', and I can't help but think… I'll need more than a tent!

I will have to think about who else to include, but I'm drawn towards the Englishman: Edwin Ray. I like his ideas, and he seems to have been working with this rather magical material, translucent concrete! It's really impressive. They cast thousands of tiny optical fibres into concrete so that it transmits either natural or artificial light, it's even possible to see colour in the light. For my own taste white light would be preferable, but this material seems to be really quite something. Sorry, I think I am becoming a little over-excited.

Back to the architects themselves, and I am tending to think that four contenders might be the right number. That might be sufficient for my needs. I'll have to give it a great deal of thought, of course, but roughly speaking, that is what I have in mind. Anyway, any further guidance will be greatly appreciated.

My love

Gaia

Letter: Carlos Santillana

Selené to Gaia

Dear Gaia,

Whilst I am delighted that you've gone for the idea of the competition, I am absolutely mortified by your attitude towards the work of Carlos Santillana! Goodness me, I am quite stuck for something to say on the matter. I can only advise that you familiarise yourself somewhat better than you are at present with this great man's *great* work. Really, I found you most dismissive. And on no account include him just to save my feelings. If he is to be included, it must be because he is 'right' to be included. I think you are out of step with quite how important this man's architectural expertise and philosophy really are. Acquaint yourself more thoroughly with his work, and we will discuss further. But when, oh when will you stop *following*, you have even used the word in your last letter. You can be quite a ninny at times. Don't follow, lead!

Edwin Ray, yes good choice. Though are you sure that material is suitable for a house? Perhaps so, I'm sceptical, but it is to be your house, and if Mr Ray is as excited as you are, who knows what might come – So, along with the Italian, that gives you two definites, Carlos as a possible, and, as you say, there must be at least one more. There is much work to be done. Get your thinking cap on, girl!

My love to you

Selené

Back at Tom's place, the days passed, Cara didn't come home, the kids didn't come home, and no one was answering his calls. Cara and the kids would come back... he expected... hoped... but he knew that it would have to be in Cara's *own good time*. – The problem with forgiving a guy when he'd done wrong, *real wrong*, was that in the act of forgiving, you were also laying the foundations for him to *do it again,* "And how's I ever gonna learn you Tom, if I don't make a stand, if I don't show you the error of your ways," she really could sound like a preacher at times, and God knows *re-lig-ion* was something she'd never been fooled by, you had to give her that at least. "If I don't show you your errors, then who the hell else is going to? Answer me that?" Like she'd give him chance to. "I said, who the hell else is going to?... No, I didn't think you'd have an answer. No good, that's what you are, no good. And if you think I'm gonna let you off lightly this time, you got it all wrong, boy. I'm staying away until you have had time to reflect on just what you have done!" What *had* he done? He could barely recall anymore. And hadn't he been punished enough already? "That was my guitar you trashed honey, my *gui-taaar!*"

Normally in these situations, when Cara upped and left, Tom could entertain himself pretty well, watching TV, maybe a few evenings with his buddies catching up on stuff: job cuts, sex, sport, and negative equity, but mostly he was consoled by his *other love... his gui-tar*. But now, the *other love* was trashed.

It was four days now, and there was still no sign of them coming home. Tom grew fretful. Naturally he didn't tell anyone what had happened, loyalty and all, so he sucked it up and suffered on his lonesome. He found himself wandering about the symmetry of the streets again, tracing repeat patterns, up and down, until, horrid déjà vu, he and Gaia backed into one another. The mailman and the widow collided, again. This time it was *him* that was falling, *his* knees, that failed.

He remembered her words:

He's dead.
He's dead, Charles.
He's dead!

The pavement, cold and damp. The scene held a horrible familiarity. He felt the blood drain from his head, he was close to passing out. Too much death. There had been too much.

Gaia knelt on one knee to steady him, poor man, what had happened to him?

"Shush, now, don't try to speak." Gently, she ran her hand across his brow, "Shush, shush." It was some minutes before he realised what had happened, if he'd had the energy, he'd have felt mightily embarrassed, but as it was, he was so wiped out he could barely muster a response.

He let the widow guide him to her place where she administered a cold flannel and offered hot tea, "Tea!" it came out all wrong, as though he was offended, he felt it sounded rude, "Sorry there Mrs Ore, can't qui-te get..."

"That's alright, take your time, get your breath. You should call me Gaia by the way, seems silly to call me *Mrs Ore*." She moved to the sink.

"Right," his tremulous response caused her to turn around.

"Are you alright Tom? It is Tom, isn't it? Not Thomas?"

"Yeah that's righ-t... just Tom."

Tom, it sounded so lovely how she said it, all soft and warm, he smiled inside.

Gaia had an idea, "I'll pop up and get my whiskey, that's what you need. It works for me! Why don't you pick out some music... take a look."

Tom glanced over at the music library, that's what it was, not a *coll-ection*, not a *sel-ection*, no, they had a LIBRARY. Wow! How cool is that, he thought. He'd noticed the music system, or part of it at least, the first time he'd been in the Construct, but he hadn't taken in this awesome LIBRARY, this was something else. This was great. His eyes widened, scanning the lists, darting back and forth in a new found mania. There was Django Reinhardt, Charlie Christian, Springsteen, Tim Buckley, Jeff Buckley – shit their lyrics were good! If anything could make a man's heart miss a beat, this could. – The guys at work said that satellite TV had some heart-stopping stuff on the more *continental* type channels – the kind of channel Cara forbid him to look at – but hell, even that stuff don't beat *mu-mu-mu-mu-sic!* Not of this calibre anyways.

Tom jumped a little as Gaia came back in.

"Sorry Tom, still rather jittery, hey? Just sit yourself down, I'll pour some of this and you tell me what you want."

"Wh-what?"

Gaia had seen that bemused expression before, it made her smile.

"Do wh-at?" he asked again nervously.

She laughed, covering her mouth with her hand, gee that was cute, he thought. Um...

"OK, don't try to speak, here, drink this," she passed him a glass of whiskey.

"Thanks, you're super kind."

"Oh, it's nothing. Think back to when I fainted on you that time..." he already had, he remembered it exactly. It had been a very big deal to him. Carrying the widow to her place; taking the keys from her pocket; taking off some of her things, though careful not to remove too many, as that would have been improper; placing her on the bed; having her drink some water; smoothing those beautiful loose curls from her face... letting her rest up some, then returning later to check she was OK, and fumbling to make his very first real coffee, hell that wasn't so difficult after all – and though connected to Charles' passing away, this had settled itself as a beautiful memory.

"So what do you want?" Gaia's words slightly startled him.

"Uh... oh, oh yeah, music, music. Don't know what's wrong with my head, a little giddy I guess. You got a great collection here."

"That's only the start of it, the rest is up in the other units."

Tom felt a slight tingling sensation, something he wasn't accustomed to around other women, women who weren't Cara, Cara or the voluptuous *Fluffy-Cream-Fairy* in the cake commercial, she was *real* sexy. Great hips, beautiful bosoms, super lips. He felt himself colour, he sank the whiskey and looked across at the bottle to distract his *too-darn-dirty-mind.* He started to wish he was a Catholic, hell, even a heathen needs to confess from time to time. Gaia ain't even my type, ain't even got that much flesh on her bones, and biggest of all, she's a *wid-ow!* What's happening to me?

"So have you decided? We must have just about anything and everything."

"Gui-tar, wonder if you have any Wes Mont-gom-ery?"

"Oh, I'm sure we do, let's have a look. And let me get you another whiskey, looks as though it's putting the colour back in your cheeks."

"No kidding." He blushed again, now afraid of his own thoughts and losing control of the words circling his brain. He clutched at the refilled whiskey tumbler, some weight in those glasses, and that was some measure of whiskey, fine stuff too.

As the Wes Montgomery found its way from hidden speakers, Tom felt the hairs rising on the back of his neck and a desperate cold shiver. Then he began to sweat.

"What is it, what's wrong?" cooed Gaia softly, moving close to him.

"My, my gui.. my gui-tar, my guitar, oh," he sobbed into her breast.

"Dear dear me, is it about your baby, is it Perry, is it an anniversary?" Was the woman deaf? Through a mix of emotions, comprising: grief at the destruction of the *other love*, grief and pain at the mention and loss of baby Perry, and then saturated in guilt that his main concern and sadness right now related to a musical instrument and not his child, he let out a pained, "It's my *GUITAR!*"

Gaia pulled back, she brushed away the fresh tears that lay on the surface of her sweater, "Your *guitar,*" she turned the music off, "I don't understand?"

"Well it's the guitar, which also means it's about Perry too, and…"

"Why don't you tell me the whole story, do you think that might help, hey?" she passed him some kitchen towel to mop up his tears.

He told her the whole story, even about buying Poochi the pit bull in the first place, and how they were gonna form a band, how long and hard he'd had to save up to buy a decent gui-tar, and then the losses, first Perry, then Poochi, and finally his *other love*. What he didn't tell her was the part that involved Cara – oh he mentioned her, but only as a fantasy *Super-Mom* character. Loyalty, it's practically a disease in some people. In any case, if he'd been totally frank, he'd have to tell her who really bought the pyjamas, explain 'why', explain 'how', explain about opening her mail! Shit! It was never ending! Them Catholics had it good. I ain't never gonna be able to get the whole-entire thing off my chest. Not ever. He explained the demolished guitar as an accident involving a reversing mail van. He was short of time, it was all he could think of, half cut with whiskey and thinking on his butt, so to speak. And it left him feeling even more guilty. His chest felt tight, thank heaven for whiskey, he drank down another in one huge gulp.

By now, Gaia was also close to tears, she needed to smoke, Tom didn't mind though he didn't like cigarettes himself. They both drank down another hefty shot of whiskey each, and brought their emotions to a comfortable state of warm inebriated numbness. "Tickles your lips does this whiskey, good stuff," said Tom.

"Yes, I don't know where I'd have been without it, well that and the kindness of a few, very special people." She smiled at him.

"*Me?*" he sounded alarmed, as though he'd been found out.

"Yes, *you*, what's so hard to believe about that?" He shrugged his shoulders still a little uncertain. "Yes, my kind mailman, I think I ought to say 'friend' by now, a friend who once rescued me from passing out in the street, and, who secretly – because maybe you think I don't notice – checks to make sure I'm still alive from time to time. I am very grateful to *you*, yes... to you... *and* to a certain pen-friend, a woman who has become an inspiration to me, a role model and more... and then I am also grateful to a certain Italian..."

"Alessandro! Oh he's great..." Tom forgot himself.

"Yes, Alessandro Cannizzaro, how do you know?"

"I..."

Gaia, solved the mystery, "You'd notice his name on my mail, of course! And it's quite a name isn't it?" She gently swirled her hand, as though writing the letters in the air, *Ale-ssan-dro Can-ni-zza-ro!*"

"Oh yes, yes! That's ju-st what I..." Tom stuttered, "and

131

yeah... it's real impressive." *Phew.* Whiskey was good like that, it could leave things very unsharp. Tom had once speculated that maybe that was why it doesn't mix so well with driving or aircraft piloting – *airline pilot,* another of Tom's fantasises.

Gaia was full of compassion for Tom, he was really quite special, and he and Cara, she supposed, probably made quite a couple. – Poor sweet lovers... all they'd been through... losing their baby like that, the dreams of starting a band. Losing the guitar itself wasn't what mattered to Tom, of course it wasn't, it was what it represented, what it would remind him of. The guitar being destroyed... well, that was just a little extra un-needed pain. A pain that was cue to deeper kinds of pain. The loss of a child, and the dreams that went along. Life was mean at times. Far too mean to some.

Gaia wasn't sure what she could do to help, but help she most certainly would. She would set aside some serious time to consider just exactly what she might do in order to help, *really help*, this man and the family he clearly adored. Wanting a whole stack of kids, and wanting to start a band, *no*, that shouldn't be too much to ask of life. Charles would also be pleased if she helped Tom; and when she'd decided just how to do this, it would be in memory of Tom and Cara's baby, Perry, and in memory of her husband:

The Architect of the Age, Charles Ore.

Perfect.

Chapter Eighteen
The Spaniard

Carlos Santillana, good architect, good husband – fertile too, the offspring that counted five, now ran to seven – twins! Good lover; good Catholic, it all added up. Oh Fabiola Santillana had her complaints, but then, who doesn't? And Fabiola's were fairly minor, mostly about Carlos not paying enough attention to his health, to his digestive system; working away from home for long stretches of time – that number of kids made for a lot of work! But when Carlos eventually received a letter from Mrs Ore, and she realised he was invited to design a house for another woman, well that was to become a sizeable complaint. It mattered little to the indomitable Fabiola that the house was for *The Architect's Widow, The Architect of the Age's widow,* so what!

"Architect's widow! *I* am an *architect's widow!* Sometimes I don't see you for months when you are off gallivanting, overseeing *this,* managing *that!* Carlos Santillana! I married you, I suffered you, I made babies for you, and *you,* what did you do, ah? You spent all your life, and *my* life, designing and building for others, and all the time I have to live in this old tumbling down thing! This… this hovel!"

Carlos responded in his usual tender-hearted fashion, "Oh don't say *hovel,* it's our home. Oh Fabi, I thought you liked it."

"*And I always… I always thought,* oh one day my sweet Carlos will surprise me and bring me to a beautiful place where he has built me a wonderful home, but no! Not you! You build for someone else. That's fine… *refugees, places troubled by war, people who had their churches bombed,* of course! Great! Fine! But now, suddenly, you want to build for someone else's *wife! Someone else's 'too rich' wife!"*

"It's a very important project, *invited* architects only, only four, I am one of only four, Fabi!"

"Everyone thinks you are oh so kind Carlos, but when you are so busy and so eager to compete with the memory and reputation of a *dead man!…* Have you stopped to think what kind of a man that makes you? I know you liked Mr Charles Ore, I know you respected him, admired him, but I also know that a part of you competes with him, even now, even though he's dead! No no no! Don't try to tell me I'm wrong. I know you, we made all these kids together, remember? 'Sensual' they call you, yes... in the bed! But *sens-i-tive*, you almost make me swear, *sensitive*, you are not. Do I have to bash you in the head to give you sense? Don't you dare build that woman a house. You build a house for *me!*"

There was nothing for it, this was going to call for a lot more loving... perhaps a new child would come. That might at least be part of the answer. The thing was, when Fabiola was pregnant, she was... she was gentle, gentle all the time. Serene. She was like that, most of the time when *not* pregnant, but periodically she could throw a wobbly, and the best way forward was to give her reason again to *coo*, to *nurture*, to be *gentle*. He was an architect, she was a mother, and best that they be provided with as much opportunity as possible to indulge in, develop, and flourish in what they were each most talented. Fabiola would agree, but there was still no escaping the question of why Carlos couldn't design a house for her... if he was to design one for anybody! Um, he would have to think about this one. Clearly, Fabiola had always applauded Carlos' architectural work; she supported him through his crises of confidence – albeit that these were few and far between; and they *had* lived in the same falling-down house since they were married, he'd just assumed she adored it as much as he did. Assumptions, he mused, not a good thing in a healthy marriage, he'd have to work something out. Fabiola was probably right (she usually was). He shouldn't build for another woman before building for his own. There was a lot of work ahead.

After much deliberation, Carlos decided to run two house design projects and he would conduct them, simultaneously! He would delegate further responsibilities in various other projects to his team, and free up more of his own precious time to work on the new house designs himself. These designs were to become truly exceptional. – Finally, there was a way forward! Besides, he missed the days when his practice was smaller, when the cut and thrust meant *eat or die*, and not meetings with financiers and investment analysts. Keep it simple! That way a man can still see what he has, still smell the air for what it is.

Carlos needed time to think, to re-engage with his ideas, to freshly acquaint himself with his own creative thoughts, and to find further inspiration. After several days of wondrous love-making, and in a suitably philosophical state, he set off – alone – for the sea.

Along the seacoast, wet sand underfoot, light wave edges rippling over toes, cooled ankles, Carlos Santillana is blissfully lost in thought. He follows the fringes of tide as they embroider the dark sand, he skips over an ambitious wave, smiling warmly as it retreats. There's a dog in the distance, exhausted with running again and again for a stick. The thrower, a child, hair blown by the wind, cheeks reddened. Carlos doesn't know the child but waves in his direction. Waves and waves. The sea, the hands. The child puts up a hand, waves back and calls something, perhaps a 'hello', but is too far away, and the wind takes all.

Carlos likes to view the world from the ground, up. He gathers up smooth and shapely pebbles, collecting them in his pockets. He moves further inland, laying down on the sand, and now the wind cannot touch him. Now the waves look different. Now, he is closer. Now, he can *see*. Architecture, for Carlos, is all about how one sees, from what position, in what direction, to what depth, in what detail, with what sensitivity. As a boy he was always most comfortable at ground level, not afraid of heights, not entirely resistant to tree climbing or scaling walls like other children, but purely on a point of preference would choose the floor as pole position. He didn't quite know why, that's just the way it was, instinctively, being close to the earth, to its rhythms, its pulse, felt right.

He imagined himself in an interview, for this was his private trick for recovering the essence of his own philosophy – and in no time at all he found himself completely absorbed, enraptured even, by his own reply to the imaginary journalist.

For me, working from the ground is very important. As an architect, I think it is very important to consider your sight line, your line of vision, for each person this is different by degree, and it will have a huge effect on the finished architecture.

Ralph Coover, for example, and in contrast to myself, always looks from high above, it's obvious to me because of the resulting architecture, and I admire it much. He creates those marvellous huge great buildings, 'landmarks' they are called, when actually it would be much more appropriate to call them sky-marks or even space-marks for they cut into... and delineate the upper space far more than they mark out the land. There is no right or wrong about these matters, they merely differ. Me, well I have a special feeling for the floor, sitting down, lying down, always close to the heart of the world, and I try to listen to it, like a mother listening to the small child she carries inside her. And when we are born, our first environmental relationship is with the floor, we explore at ground level, we crawl before we walk, and so meet the space higher up only later on. For me, keeping in touch with the earth, the human condition, with the basic senses, with simplicity... this instructs all my work, but maybe I just never developed very far as a human being, and only someone like Coover or even Cannizzaro, yes, maybe from the womb they came out walking! Or flying even! They are more advanced perhaps, and perhaps so their architecture! But of course, I don't believe that last part at all, not at all!

He purrs with laughter. The purr becomes a contented roar.

Atmospheric conditions, wind loads, variations in temperature, the relationship of the architecture to its foundations and to the earth, quite literally, I almost think of my architecture as something organic, like a child growing in the womb, leaving the womb, but somehow always attached. Yes, my architecture is something like that, growing out of the landscape, out of the soil, the rock, the sand. The sand.

He shivers now, the light is fading, a shadow moves over him like a sundial, it is the child smiling. The boy.

It's been a long time since Carlos' last interview, he's been too busy, but he quite relishes them, and thinks now, that he must indeed accept the next good invitation to talk about his work, his thoughts now clearer. The boy is still standing over him. "Are you dead?"

"No, can't you see my eyes moving?"

"I can now, but just now you looked straight out, like a dead man."

"What a relief for you!" Carlos gets up, smiles and dusts off the sand that's gathered over him, "Can't have been very nice thinking you'd seen a corpse!"

"That's OK, I like dead stuff."

Carlos laughs and pats the boy on the shoulder.

Chapter Nineteen
The Competition

For the first time in her life Gaia was up against a truly substantial challenge, and this all of her own making. The results would likely shape the rest of her life, and influence, if not change, the lives of several others. She wasn't entirely aware how far-reaching the consequences might be – but that was doubtless a good thing, for had she been, she would unquestionably have given up, lacking the necessary level of self-belief, the natural coward resurfacing.

Back in the US, Ralph Coover had plenty to say on the subject of what *lies ahead*, "Yup, that's the beauty of the future, few can foresee it or *read* it, whatever that's supposed to mean. The future, well, it just plain happens!" He prided himself on living in the present, "Seems logical is all, in this god-forsaken land," and the only churches or temples he was interested in were those erected in *the Architect's Name*, usually his. But then *Bigger and Better* was by now pretty much his catchphrase, and like a laughing baboon he added, "Hell, if I could see into the future and had any idea of just how much I could get away with, then shit, I'd just have to push it and get away with a shit-load more!" Ultimately Ralph was far more easily seduced by power than by women, "And thank goodness it's that way," he hollered, "ain't enough space for two insatiable bedroom-types, eh Zandro?"

Gaia took her time in deciding the final two candidates to invite to the competition. As Charles' widow, she had more than a keen knowledge of the major players' work, but more new names were emerging, and these were responsible both for phenomenal moves in the design of the more modest and medium-sized projects such as schools, galleries, bridges and the like, as well as the ever higher and more spectacular visions that were raising the stakes on the skyscraper front. They all demanded serious consideration. It was a time of unparalleled architectural talent, previously unimaginable feats of engineering, and ingenious technological breakthrough. There was no dismissing the *mise en place* achieved in Spain, Italy, Norway and Switzerland; and no ignoring what was going up in Saudi Arabia, Indiana, Malaysia, Japan and Singapore. Skylines shifted ever upwards, nudging moon and stars, splicing up the air-space like sabres, pushing ordinary aircraft into outer space, frightening the wind out of weather fronts. Well... almost. *Truly*, as Coover put it, *things are getting wild!*

The more Gaia investigated, the harder she found it to decide. Just when she thought she had settled on three architects and almost a fourth, a fifth would seem to elbow their way in. And then a sixth. What to do? Replace the third architect with another? Include one more? Have five contenders? Six? – What certainly wasn't up for debate was the degree of vigour with which Gaia took on this challenge. The more she researched, the more intense her excitement, the more impassioned she became, the more revitalised.

But one thing was as true as it had always been, that an architect's prime goal was to design the private house, a wonderful private house, usually their own, and winning a commission such as this, from the widow of one of the world's greatest, just upped the ante that little bit further.

A few more anxious and excited days would follow before Gaia made her final selection, four world class architects, all with different philosophical leanings, arguably disparate tastes, but with an equal measure of architectural passion and creative verve, and all capable of innovative genius. And so, the final list emerged. The competition would be open to: *Theoretical Architect,* Edwin Ray; Alessandro Cannizzaro, *the Italian,* famous for dictating the *Perfect Site; Sensual Builder,* Carlos Santillana; and *Bigger and Better,* Ralph Coover of *Ideal Context* infamy.

Letter: Decided!
Gaia to Selené

Dear Selené,

I am sorry I have only written brief notes these past months, but as you rightly suggested, there has been much work to do. Now I have plenty to share with you, and I can't begin to tell you what a transformation I have just undergone. Inspirational! I've attended lectures, visited sites, offices and openings, it has been a kind of madness, almost. But finally I have worked out the final four to invite to the competition. You cannot say I ignore your advice, nay bossiness!

Don't follow, lead!

And lead, I jolly well will.

I have perfected the art of the 'list', and believe I have included four architects of diverse taste and inclination, and most importantly, of the highest possible calibre. They do however have certain things in common, and these are prerequisites of mine, the most important being their commitment to, and understanding of, what is required for true quality of life... for each in their own ways appreciates balance; each looks for simplicity and clarity... and it seems to me... they do so... with heart.

As proof of my leadership, I have already written the letters of invitation requesting their design proposals – at last, a house for myself! Of the four letters there is only one variation, in that addressed to Alessandro Cannizzaro, as I have finally accepted his invitation to visit. Don't misunderstand me, I will not develop any favouritism, and intend to judge the proposals fairly.

I am so excited now, I can barely wait to see what they come up with! Heavens, look at me, so seduced and preoccupied by this venture, I am almost forgetting to list the architects for you. They will be:

America's Ralph Coover
Italy's Alessandro Cannizzaro
Spain's Carlos Santillana
United Kingdom's Edwin Ray

An impressive list I think you'll have to agree, and hardly the work of a *ninny!*

The architects will all be informed of the names of the other contenders, and I will ask that each provide a model of their design. I will allow ten weeks as the deadline. I think you'll agree that seems reasonable. I know the models take time, but I also want to inject a sense of tension, positive tension, and urgency, into the work. I know that Charles always worked best and produced his most impressive work with his back against the wall.

I want to offer them as open a remit as possible, I want them to feel a sense of adventure and freedom in this endeavour, but it is important to me that the dwelling is of modest proportions, I am so weary of this huge lonesome Construct and its sterile air.

I am dying to hear what has become of the *horseman,* please tell.

I hope this finds you well, dear Selené.

My sincere love to you

Gaia

Letter: Carlos Santillana

Selené to Gaia

Dear Gaia,

Look at you madam! Practically risen from the ashes, if that isn't too insensitive a thing to say? Gosh, moves, yes, and what moves you make! Marvellous, you could not have made me happier, my dear. Very good choices you have made. Charles would be proud, and I am delighted, though I continue to stress that this whole endeavour must be with *you* at the helm and at its centre, it is after all, for your home. Everyone has their 'time' in life, we know quite well that Charles, and rightly so, had his. You my dear, have been overlooked it seems, perhaps now, is your chance. This time, my sweet, is for you.

The 'horseman', golly what to tell. A consummate and passionate lover, but alas, somewhat... clingy, yes, that's the word. I have had to dispense with his talents. It's simply no good when my lovers become silly. It was short and desperately sweet, but there we are, it is over.

My love to you

Selené

Gaia was pleased at Selené's approval, she lit a cigarette in satisfa[...]
and looked over her list.

house
lover
Italy

Designs for the 'house' would soon be under way; Gaia was about to
visit Italy; 'lover' she pondered. Why did I leave 'lover' there? She was
about to strike it out with her pen – it was just a word – she relented
and left it untouched. She left her desk, and packed. In her luggage,
she included a few of Selené's letters, it seemed they had assumed the
level of protective talisman, and it was also a means of taking Selené
with her in spirit since all else was out of the question. From her store
of correspondence she selected particular letters, landmarks so to say,
and these included the inimitable 'final three' from Selené to Charles,
for these had been her first introduction to Selené, and they reminded
Gaia of how easy it was to get things wrong, how awry things go
when too much is imagined, and how necessary it was to retain the
skill of laughing at her own temporary madness, lest it take up more
permanent residence.

   Without thought, the *rosy-jamas* found their way into the nightwear
section of her very ordered packing, and soon things were set. She
would travel in casual clothes: jeans, T-shirt and hiking boots – the
leather boots had softened up nicely as testament to their lengthy
service. All packed, and Italy was finally to become a reality!

Chapter Twenty
Italy

Alessandro received his invitation to the competition, and as if that wasn't sufficiently pleasing, the widow had accepted his offer of hospitality – OK, so it had taken longer than he'd hoped, but now, finally, she was on her way! Well, of course! His pride never far from the surface. And suddenly he could indulge in an *everything's going my way*, kind of feeling. It wasn't quite *"Bravo! Oh Mama!"* – not quite yet, but he felt sure that it was getting that way.

Having let fantasy get the better of him – 'Gaia', a svelte curly-haired Marilyn, stylishly attired, perhaps Prada, Gucci, a stunning suit at least, gorgeous shirt, shoes… perhaps by Jimmy Choo, a sexy, quietly confident look – imagine his distress at the dishevelled reality.

Worst of all, my God! – What has she on her feet? Is that possible? My little angel in *rock-climbing-carcasses!* He realised that for the magazine pictures, of course, the stylists had taken care of everything. Could her own sense truly be quite so *off*, even the jeans were not stylish, it's quite difficult to get even jeans wrong! But then again, she was in a state of grief, she had let things go, let 'practical' run roughshod over the 'aesthetic', but really, honestly speaking, what had her delicate little feet been – captured by? He blamed her late husband entirely, for *loving her so little!* Really, this was a crime. He had a lot of work to do. He scoffed now as he thought of Charles. He couldn't help himself and hugged Gaia tightly, almost forgetting to let go. What an extraordinary woman, reduced to… to *ordinary!* It was criminal! The tragedy of being loved so little – but the contrast would be to his credit. And he was determined to do some good.

Just think, soon, in my hands, she will be a goddess, she will be as beautiful as nature and fashion intended, as loved as no other, and as happy, well, perhaps only she can measure that part, but at any rate, I will make her much happier than she has been with that neglectful husband! But really, you cannot blame, there are some things for which certain men have no talent. Charles! That's just how it is.

Alessandro was flattered to be included in the competition, though he secretly wished she would just forget it and commission him directly, or better still, just plain move in with him. Why not? His place was palatial, and some day, when all other architectural challenges had been met, he would design something in the manner of a new home that was both palatial and paradisiacal, what else?!

He escorted his guest around the rooms he'd had prepared for her, each decorated in a very simple manner, light block colour, plenty of natural light coming in, she liked it. And the atmosphere? One of tenderness and ease.

Vast windows opened out to distant views... a surge of rock, seemingly frozen, white at the top; a middle distance of town life, church spires and rooftops; and close by... bold lines of trees, green and grey.

Standing in the warmth... spots of colour danced in the sun, sand and ochre yellow, bright blues, red; the air... light and fresh. The dwelling and its owner delivering a mood of quiet serenity and seemingly without effort.

Outside, pathways meandered easily around fertile gardens. Inside, the morning light held a gentle quality, drops of gold and red wine sunlight hung in Gaia's bedroom, and in a blink were gone. They might come again tomorrow...

Here she could relax. Here she could breathe. – By her bed... a small square table. On the table was a house built of bread. A small wooden figure stood at its door. The figure was a penguin. Gaia smiled. A small bread house. A small wooden penguin.

She slept.

After a few restful days, Alessandro began his campaign, not only to cheer Gaia, but to woo her. He would leave the re-attiring until later, some things require a sense of right timing and subtlety, Gaia would not too easily be won, and for the world he would not be heavy-handed in this matter. Oh, the boots would have to go, yes, but this would have to be played out tenderly – in any case those *rock-climbing-carcasses* were practically the living dead, he fantasised that they might just up and leave of their own accord. Re-cladding those delicate feet would mark his coming in for the passionate kill, and that could only happen when the time was right. For the moment, he must content himself with preparing the ground, and he pursued this wisely and gently, with care, with tenderness; the finest restaurants – and a natural charisma.

"Alessandro, you have the reputation of an almost maverick architect!" Gaia broke off, and for a brief moment she was somewhere else, she returned to the present near to laughing, "And certainly among other leading architects, you are talked about incessantly! I have even heard of you spoken of as a heretic! What do you make of that?"

"To be honest, I think that is exactly what is in my favour. Those architects with a rather more conservative outlook, perhaps they are also those who are a little bit afraid, and so they call my architecture *novelty architecture, inconsequential architecture* and so on, 'inconsequential' – why such a big word to say nothing? I have read such things in magazines, in the papers. It's funny for me, that these others who are world class architects in their own right would use up time in an interview of their own to talk so much about me! Wow! That feels *so* good! You can't imagine just how good. – More wine?" A divine wine was poured and savoured.

Gaia was intrigued. Alessandro's vitality was potent, but she, not easily seduced. "Anyway Gaia, for me, these architects are afraid. I always divide people into those who are afraid, and those who are not. I've done that since I was fifteen years old and it works. Me, I'm not afraid of anything, if you like you can call it being brave. The thing is, you need some talent, but actually, more than that, it is about stamina, and hard work. It's that simple. And come on now, all those who have gone before us, they helped make it easy for the next generations. What have we to be afraid of? Adolf Loos introduced great functional, un-messy, unadorned architecture for us, so you got the fundamentals of the modern age from him pretty much. And also you have Gropius, Le Corbusier, some others." Tactically, he steered clear of mentioning more contemporary architects by name, almost as though they didn't exist, that the landscape was now almost entirely his to design. Privately he admired many, but he would rarely give breath to their names.

"That wonderful English woman, Eileen Gray, she did some brave work in the 1920s, of course you know, I'm sure. She said... she said... that... *To create, one must first question everything,* and she was quite correct." He knocked the ash from his cigarette. "I really admire her – Corbusier, he was a cheeky guy, once he painted some kind of mural on the walls of her home, without asking! He is someone I admire for sure, but that was too much! He was a bit of a dog sometimes. She said he was a vandal. That's not a good way to be with a woman. No no no. I learned that story as a little boy from my father, and my father called our dog after him because it always pissed up the walls – Anyway, Eileen Gray, she really had vision – because, Gaia, women can do it too! But most of you still don't realise it. – And now world, you got ME! How lucky you are. I don't claim to have so much in common with that Austrian, Loos, but really, you have to admit, he must have been a great guy. And sticking up his two fingers at all that fussy ornamentation, well for that, we have to thank him. Anyway, all these architects today, well, there's so much great work about, but for me, when it's *me* who will be interviewed, I'm telling you, I just talk about *me, me, me, me, me!* And I savour *ev-er-y* word." And with that he kissed his fingers in the manner of a large contented chef, "*Sat-is-fac-tion,* yes!"

Gaia remained silent, he wondered what she might be thinking? The wine was taking effect on both, and Alessandro felt further challenged, to enchant, "In life, it is possible to be many things, and of course that depends on your background, your chances, choices, but it is only possible to be truly excellent at one thing. That is what I believe. To excel at one thing, that is a possibility for everyone, *re-garrrrd-less* of anything. If you want it, bad enough, for sure, you will get it. Nothing as certain as that, and those who don't get it, who whinge and whine: *oh but I was born into the wrong family; my brother got all the chances; no one guided me when I was young; the politics of my country prevented it; I was born into the wrong class; I had a bad mother,* oh I've heard it all, and I tell you, none of these is a reason for not succeeding, not a one,

147

ultimately. There are ways around every problem. Look back through history and you see it everywhere. The important thing to realise is that the only thing that can really hold you back is *your-self*. Those who don't get where they want, or what they want, simply didn't want it bad enough!"

"You really believe that?"

"It's not a matter of belief, I know it! I am the proof of it, but enough of this subject eh? We are getting too serious, paddling in murky waters. – Another drink? Here, let's dip our feet in something closer to champagne? – In fact, let's do it. I will order some! Excuse me, waiter!"

A youthful chubby waiter gazed back over his shoulder and blushed as his eyes met Alessandro's, then the curly-haired cherub distantly mouthed that he would be over directly to take the order. Gaia is less easily won than this innocent male, and Alessandro knows it. She picks up the conversation, "If you could have been anything, why did you settle on architect?"

"Settle! That's a funny word, you think there might be something better? No there is not! I clearly chose architecture. You want to know why? That's quite fascinating to me, indulge me, it's sexy." He was in his element now, "Yes architecture is so very sexy to me. Please, excuse me just a moment. – Yes waiter, champagne, Veuve Clicquot. Thank you." He smiled but briefly, he must not lose Gaia's attention, "That great photographer, Cartier… Bresson, he captured what they all famously quote as 'the decisive moment', a great achievement. In its way. The singular, short-lived, genius, the 'moment'. But for the architect these moments are many, continuous, extended if you like." Was he losing her? He was conscious of trying too hard. He would say something gauche, crude even, just to draw her back, to see her pupils dilate, put some colour in those too white cheeks. OK, so it was rather childish, boyish, but only tongue-in-cheek, and it might work! So why not? – "In so many professions – how shall I say? Well… let's just say that they finish short, while the architect's orgasm… this really fulfils, really travels, and first class too!" His words culminating in an efflorescence of self-satisfied charismatic laughter and followed up as though he were Mozart in composition of flight,

by a flurry of flirtatious expressions, blossoming cheekily into, "Oh!
I can hardly believe I said that, but actually I mean it. Implicitly. So
don't waste your time with men in other professions – when it comes
to lovers, you can't beat architects, and certainly not THE ITALIAN
ARCHITECT!"

"And when it comes to architects? Which one cannot be
bettered?"

"Ah, *Gai-a*, I don't even hear your question! For that, you certainly
know the answer."

Chapter Twenty-one
Cara Came Home

Cara wasn't sure what she believed anymore, and if she was to take her mother's advice – *heaven forbid* – then she'd leave this no-good man and find herself a new one. See, the thing was, when push came to shove, Cara knew that there wasn't any better than Tom Bradshaw. She knew he wasn't bad, at least not *that* bad, and she also knew from previous experience that no one *but* Tom Bradshaw was likely to put up with her vicious temper; her constant revision of rules, 'interminable double standards' being her particular speciality. In terms of the balance of power however, she knew that the right way to handle a man was never to let on that she was aware of *any* of this. Blinkered, that was Tom Bradshaw, and that's how he needed to stay.

Cara came back with the kids while Tom was out at work. She'd missed him, and the kids had *really* missed him, they were each of them daddy's girl, daddy's boy. Cara hated how he was favourite with them, but today, well, it was OK, and she *had* destroyed his guitar. Hell, it was only an accident really, and he shouldn't go leaving his stuff lying around like that, a person could have a bad fall. She wasn't good at facing up to the truth, it hurt. Anyway, it was just a silly old guitar, they could save and get him another one or put it on credit. Cara had always liked the idea of the family band, despite her disapproval of it being named after their dopey-old-dog. It could just have easily been called: *Cara's Crew,* or *Cara and the Kids*, or *Cara*'s *Cradle* or… anything! Cara wasn't musical, but they just couldn't tell her, deep down she knew it herself, but so what, that was all the more reason to use her name for the band, shit, she ought to be included somehow! That was only right and fair, "But Ma, you're always telling us *life isn't fair, so just plain get on with it!"* Kids! She blamed the teachers. No manners these days, no manners at all, Tom ought to realise what a tough time she had! Delivering mail! Huh! And now she was faced with a huge pile of mail, much of which was addressed to her, and most of which heralded a new level of truth facing. Credit card debt and catalogue overdue notices, hers and hers alone. What to do? Well anyway, they really had needed new stuff, most kids had several pairs of Nikes these days, not her fault. It was about time she had new clothes, having kids makes a woman lose her figure and she was plain *too busy* to get it back, wasn't like they were the sort to have gym membership for Christ's sake, and face it, that *would* cost. Tom should be grateful. A delivery van arrived. A new sofa, *new sofa!* Oh! She'd totally forgotten that one. She signed, they removed the old one – all part of the service – and planted the new one in its grave. She shivered. It was all too much, she had to get out, besides, they needed some shopping. Food. She ought to buy some food, poor Tom, he was probably skin and bones, having been left all alone. A good fry-up. That would fix things. She set out to the supermarket, listing… bacon, eggs, tomatoes, mushrooms, bread, butter, and fresh coffee as Tom had recently taken a liking to that, God knows how, but never mind that, and sugar. Keep him sweet.

Tom collected his paycheque, the guys were all looking downhearted. Rumours were circulating. Redundancies. A new take-over. It was unavoidable. Still, he might be one of the lucky ones.

There are few things than can make a man weep like an old woman, one of them is facing the loss of a half-decent income, another is facing his wife and mother of his children with such news, and another is facing the bills she's stacked up.

Not even *Tom Jones* could have handled that lot much better.

Tom knew she'd cooked the fried stuff specially, to say sorry, but he just couldn't stomach it, and he didn't want to cry in front of the kids. *New sofa! More Nikes! What!* When women punish with shopping, that can really hurt. He went straight out again, wandered the streets. Redundancy. Hell, it probably wouldn't come to that, had to be just rumours, he'd probably be 'retained', after all, he was 'time-served' as Cara put it – diplomacy – after all, this was a woman with a stack of unpaid bills stuffed in the kitchen drawer.

Sometimes, all the streets, the sky, people passing by, the air even, it was concrete, all of it. Some people get a run of bad luck, and some people get a *dumper-truck-load* of concrete poured right down their throat 'till they're full to choking. *Fuck!* He sank to the ground, head in hands. What to do?

Chapter Twenty-two
Alessandro Cannizzaro, Eyrie

Alessandro invited Gaia to stay on in Italy for as long as she wished, for the full ten weeks until the competition deadline, *longer*, whatever would make her happy. She could, of course, take her time to think it over... for sure, there was no need to rush and decide anything. But oh, that she would rush!

Being in his company was easy; the competition was set and running; Italy was brimming with romance and distraction, so why not stay? Spontaneity was exciting, but still, it did not come as naturally to Gaia as she might have liked. She would take a little time to think it through.

For the first few days Gaia had come down to breakfast wearing the *rosy-jamas*. Alessandro never commented, and Gaia soon realised that it had to be his modesty that prevented him acknowledging the gift – she felt suddenly gauche at her insensitivity, it would have been more appropriate to get fully dressed, and spare his shyness. She would do so from now on. *Modesty! Shyness! Alessandro! No...*

The following morning Gaia appeared at the breakfast table fully dressed as planned. This raised a smile and her host remarked, "Oh, I see the night-suit is gone!" He was so pleased that she was no longer wearing the dreadful English pyjamas, "You sleep naked now perhaps in this Italian heat! That's good, me too," he laughed, "and for that reason I don't frighten you with my own night-time attire at breakfast! That would be too much ah?!" Gaia couldn't follow him entirely, and it would never have crossed her mind that the pyjamas were not in fact Alessandro's kindness, but that of another. For once, Tom Bradshaw's endeavours would remain concealed.

Back home, Tom knew the 'law of averages' had to kick into action sooner or later, and things surely had to start going his way again. That was Tom, always the optimist. Unfortunately, he would never get to know just how big a success the *rosy-jamas* had been. And far more unfortunately, redundancy papers were soon to hit the doormat —*the law of what?*

Alessandro took on the challenge of the competition with heart, interrupting the project only to entertain or guide his house guest. He would design her a house, a home, and what a place it would be. He kept all his design ideas secret from her, but each day would replace the bread residence beside her bed with a new one. The small penguin standing close, and this carved as skilfully as each small bread house was realised. A master craftsman by now, Alessandro indulged his childhood building pleasure still.

Gaia would spend her days keeping a notebook and reading; taking walks; chatting in a smattering of Italian with anyone she met; admiring Alessandro… touched by his attention and pleased by the time alone whilst he worked. A comfortable balance seemed to emerge. Separate endeavours by day and the subtle move to seek the other's company at dusk and dawn. – A small wooden penguin found another on a broad oriental table, and home-made sushi was shared by four. – *Would she stay a little longer? Until the competition? He would like to help her choose a good location for the competition finale… but didn't want to presume. They could have it there! In Italy! He had plenty of rooms, and the gardens… they could all be his guests! Or… he could book hotel rooms, yes, that might be better. Whatever she thought was best. But perhaps he was speaking too much… but if he could help he would, and if she would stay he would be…*

"Yes, Alessandro, I will stay. I would love to stay."

Self-conscious and happy, he tilted the penguins. "Hurrah!" they seemed to call, "Hurrah!"

At times Alessandro felt Gaia to be quite vulnerable, and he would dream of her home as a place of safety and calm; but then she was its opposite and he must not mistakenly design something of a cage for one who must most certainly feel at ease, without even walls to hold her! Why suddenly so dramatic? He thought of his mother, looking into her photograph now for inspiration, guidance, approval. He looked at one of the small penguins returned to his desk, but no response. He might carve a wise owl. He sighed, and put the penguin to one side. This deepening affection for Gaia was testing him. He must not let it put him off his stride, but turn it into strength! Building for one he was now coming to love.

He sketched with his paint box, drawing out images of house designs in light-touch watercolour. *And how to find... how to create, the perfect dwelling?* What is its shape? Where to begin?

The Orient!
   Mountains!
      Hideaways!

Ideas running, entangling, rising. More paper! More water! More mountains! And higher! Like an eagle's nest, cliff edge, mountain top – he lost himself in the imagery of Oriental paintings and the dwellings of poets and priests escaping to inaccessible, almost imperceptible structures. Settings where they would find ease, where they would be inspired, where they would enjoy the passion and succour of nature.

Huangshan! The Yellow Mountains of China, Anhui province – he had never been, and yet he felt he had. He spent hours, days, studying prints, paintings and sketches of Huangshan. He immersed himself in the magic of the poetry written in those mountains, and of those mountains, reaching high above clouds, nudging the sky, soft yellow rock, peak after peak after peak, formed in the images of nature. Natural sculptures. In stone, a turtle, a rabbit, a lotus flower. And these emerging at the least accessible points, the settings so beautiful a man might weep. Staring back into the paper now... the colours began to settle, and if he looked just hard enough, he could make out a few delicate structures of his own... perhaps a temple; a home sculpted in poetry; a painter's sanctuary; a writer's nest – a timber frame... a bamboo cradle. He would consider the quality of light, the quality of sound... the quality of silence.

Alessandro again took up his paintbrush and sketched, now frantically, fluently, the design coursing through his veins.

A small temple.
A dwelling.
An eyrie.

Chapter Twenty-three
Carlos Santillana, Sensual Stone

Fabiola was soon pregnant again, and Carlos at ease, lost in fresh and fabulous thoughts of architecture, and that as much a child and as dear to him as those at varying heights around his feet, and the precious new twins, and the seed just sown. Two houses. Each with the aura of his love locked deep into the design. He watched his children now running back and forth, into the house, and out again, attached to their parents, and not... part of the house and the landscape, but free. Pebbles, he mused, taking up some of his collection from his solitary beach escapade and examining them closely.

My children, my houses... They are not sand, subject to the conditions of the weather, too easily compressed into the ground by the weight of lashing and relentless rains, restrained, or else easily dried out in the heat and blown hither and thither. No. They are not sand. He paused. And they are not rocks, too heavy, inflexible, immovable, easily chipped and scarred. They are not rocks. Pebbles, he rubbed one gently between finger and thumb. Smooth, perfect, each with its own identity... with an essential innocence, a gentleness... but with definition, with shape. Pebbles. My children are like pebbles! *I will design two houses, I will design two new children, two precious pebbles!* Huge structures whose form will be that of two perfect pebbles; and not stone, but clad in wood. He remembered the boat-builders he had once met on his travels... their skills he had much admired. Ideas! Ideas!

Perfectly smooth, undulating forms in wood, no awkward joins, craftsmanship of the highest degree; and if the Spanish were not expert enough in this, then he would search further. Norway, there certainly they would have such skills. It was all possible, realisable, passionful. Perfectly smooth forms.

Where the light would naturally distinguish particular areas of the surface would be the points informing the positions for window panes set flush to the body of the building, expertly moulded, seamlessly married to a surface of almost liquid wood. A door, *two*, again handcrafted, following the pebbles' natural and subtle curves and cleverly gliding inward, inviting guests to the centre, the heart. A pebble, a heart, the small beating hearts of the sea – pebbles. Happily, he inhaled deep, and let out a satisfied cry.

He was about to rise and wander about in the remaining sunlight out of doors when Fabiola called him, she knew exactly what he was about to do, *go missing*, and there was much to do at home! Restraining food was served up, it was a wonderful ritual, they smiled at one another, she knowingly, he, caught out. From the doorway he called to the children to come in and undress for bed. He could take his walks in the morning. She was right.

Chapter Twenty-four
Ralph Coover, Fear before Genius

Shit, I never been asked to design something as *iddy-biddy* as a house before. Hell, I build big! This darn competition thing, well... it's making me nervous. That's women for yer, that's why I steer clear of 'em mostly, despite what ole Zandro's always telling me. Women are trouble. Hell, can't she just get herself a row house or somethin', or whatever else they live in over there. Shit, she could afford to buy herself a whole big, enormous castle on what old Ore would have left her, a whole heap of castles! Isn't that the thing with the English, I mean, isn't that the whole problem with their modern architecture, they're always kinda stuck, stuck on old ideas. Yup! It's like they can't help it. They like all that old stuff – so why can't she just go ahead and buy somethin' Georgian for Christ's sake! Least that shit's pretty.

For Ralph, nothing could put him off his stride quite like a woman could, and for some reason, he found himself completely overwhelmed by the idea of designing for this particular woman. In Ralph's fertile imagination Gaia had assumed skyscraper intensity, taken on an unreasonable quota of awe, and was pretty much paralysing his take on reality. Stupid really, but heck, it can take the best of 'em that way at times, even the maestro, *Bigger and Better*.

Hell, I got myself so used to living in just two rooms mostly, hotel rooms at that, not even rooms designed by me! Just two rooms and a closet! Spend most of my time making a home of such rooms, working on site most of the time, overseeing my scraper projects, shit, I never even thought of designing houses... a home, not even for myself. Maybe that's it! After all, that's what most architects dream of, most *normal* architects, and they leave off of doing it for as long as hell 'cos they know that's gonna be the ultimate leveller, that'll be what you're most harshly judged for, never mind what the hell else you build! Finally, the real day of reckoning comes, and you find yourself most brutally judged, by EVERYONE over a *house!* Shit, I'm just yella!

Just plain, yokey-ole-yellow, a coward. Oh man, I gotta get out, clear my brain, get some freakin' bourbon down my gullet. Guess I'd better put some pants on. This is a tough one. *A house!* – sweet Jesus, now where's my darn disco pants hiding their 'selves?

It's all Zandro's fault anyways, gotta be. She's a visiting him, he's out to do his romancing on her, Jees-us, why the hell can't she just go ahead and move into his place? Ain't no fathoming women. No fathoming at all.

Ralph figures that it must be down to Alessandro that the site for the house isn't fixed, but that part at least, he approves of. He pulls on his too-tight, red velvet flares, perhaps for inspiration – well, denying the lower half of the body its blood supply, and forcing it all to concentrate around the brain might be Ralph's route to great ideas, but it might also answer for the lack of action seen by the contents of those pants.

All dressed up, Ralph set off out in search of some serious night life and *did his thing* – he was something of a *secret* disco dancer; he never minded people hearing him sing along to Motown, but dancing, that was quite a different matter. Ralph, hiding his dancing light under a bushel – not so his architectural! Hours later, he danced back to his hotel room, half cut, and just as he turned on the light, he'd got it.

Yo! Take a 1970s disco glitter-ball, the kind that spin overhead covered in all those tiny mirrored tiles, a globe… with a real sparkly skin… wow… yeah! Make it gigantic, like *gi-gan-tic*… set it next to the sea, part of it cut into the land, part submerged in the water, a little ways… sink some real heavyweight anchorage to hold it there nice and steady – we'll figure something, easy does it – oh hell, this is great! –and with the tide lapping there… I suggest, at full tide… to approximately one third the height of the globe. Big shiny globe! *Man!* I'll have the ball clad in nice reflective panels that don't allow outsiders to see in, and vary those the dweller can see out of… yup! And the part that's swimming, 'swimming' get that! – I like this idea, I like it a lot. Well, it ain't gonna be wobbling around, I want it not only to be secure, but totally still… but I simply *have* to have part of it in the waves, I just have to – Anyway, the 'swimming part' as I'm liking to call it, from there you'll be able to look out to sea. Yeah, part 'in' the water, looking out 'on' the water, how cool is that? The sun beating down, glistening on it sometimes; or snow flakes dancing around. – Waves lapping against the sides, shit, an amazing seascape as the view! Sometimes calm and dreamy, sometimes wild and crazed! Darn I like this place.

I'm gonna design it the coolest curviest glass bathtub, spliced through to meet with the curve of the glass globe wall, so it'll look and feel just like you're bathing right out in the sea itself, oh I'm on a roll alright. – just undo these here pants a little, *phew*, either they's a shrinking or this little ole gut's busting out further than I realised.

Of course the structure'll need to be large enough to accommodate floors, two I guess; with the entrance being high up, reached by a super gyring cantilevered staircase! How about that? Shit! I want it for myself! – Nope. No good being selfish. The lady needs cheering up, and shit, if living in a gigantic disco ball don't do it, nothing will!

Take a look at me! Gee! All that moping around, all that: *oh, I can't do it, I can't design a house,* what's wrong with me? *Man!* Just a drop of bourbon, put on my disco pants and hell! Eureka! That's the fundamentals covered. She's a nice woman wanting a cool house, and hell is she gonna get one!

Ralph reflects for a moment on Alessandro.

I feel pretty bad about this Zandro my pal, but I think I got you licked on this one. Nothing like a little *iddy-biddy* shot of fear to kick ass, and hell, out pops *gee-ni-us!* Huh! *Cutting-edge-freakin-transitional-archi-tarti-tecture!* Look out world, here come Coover's Balls! And that's only just the start.

A fresh glass of bourbon in hand, swivelling on his heels, his own sweet take on Motown swirling round his head:

Ain't no stopping me now!
I'm on the move!
Ain't no stoppin me now!
I've got the groove!

161

Chapter Twenty-five
Edwin Ray, Passion and Spittle

Edwin Ray is secretly delighted by the competition, but he needs a certain amount of time to play out his pretence at resistance. It's three in the morning, he paces about his architecture laboratory in short measured steps, almost tripping as his mind outruns his tread. He mutters away to himself, gradually growing in spirit and spittle, building up to a rant with arms a waving, and celebrating the challenge with red-wine cork a popping. His trusty dog, The Scotsman, has been awake and observing for a while now. He's seen the signs before. It might not be tonight, but soon something magical will emerge.

For the moment this project seems inconceivable. Where to start? No distinct site. Few points of reference. Some details, requirements, yes... but almost a free hand. Can this be true? Should he contact Mrs Ore? Enquire further? But this largely open brief is surely what she desires, it must indeed be her intention. And he would not want to bother her, she is still perhaps in mourning after all. Each of the other architects will have been furnished with just as few details; and for all the world he would not care to give the impression that the task belied his capabilities. So few restrictions! He *should* be in his element! This, he knew. But still, he muses, one cannot start from nowhere! How to begin? Damn and blast! *Argh! So many questions! Must not pull out my beard!* The Scotsman rests his head on one side, he knows that Edwin begins with a rant and ends with design, 'tis always the way. Though it will certainly take time.

Edwin taps his pencil rhythmically, runs an aria through his head, strokes his beard... mindful not to pull. Music! Now therein lies stimulus aplenty! He reaches out, makes a selection and presses 'play'. Inspired, he sups a little more on a rather fine wine... *music*... is this the initial inroad? Or a diversion? Too soon to tell. – And materials! I will allow these to inform in some measure... yes, I will work that way... there is much to do, much indeed, and time, just ten weeks!

And she wants a model! She doesn't ask for much! – *The wine, the music – inspiration, ah! – Charles' love of opera!* That's certainly an inroad! A musical score! Perhaps something can be mapped, charted from... from an opera score, yes. Charles Ore was quite passionate about opera, it was well known. Perhaps his wife's passion also! For who does not love opera? I must do some research. An opera, possibly the libretto itself... that could really form the textural dimension. Much to do, to do!

Edwin slapped his thigh in satisfaction, nothing like a challenge to set the adrenaline pumping, that and a soupcon of wine – a whole bottle by sunrise. He toyed with ideas the night through.

Somehow, he reflected, the place must also draw together the Ores' lives... his great life and then parting from this world, and her emergence from grief – for that is surely what inspired her to come up with the competition at all – his passing away, and her movement forwards and into a new future.

He scribbled some notes... A lexicon of life, then death, its aftershocks, the life that continues. There is so much to consider. But music... always with music....

A taste for smart concrete at least, something our work had in common, so it would be nothing of a betrayal of my own work, and could very well form something of a compliment to Charles. Or perhaps, translucent concrete? Nice indeed... but again, too early to say.

Edwin would give it some thought.

Glass... a glass roof, for Gaia Ore might well be suited to a dwelling with a feeling of serenity, artfulness, and simplicity... and she would need light... as much natural light as could possibly be drawn in. – A model... maybe so, but I want this project animated, in fact, I want the most marvellous computer animation of this work possible! Let's work at this like nothing else!

Music, was indeed, ultimately the key, though not quite in the way he had first envisaged. The Scotsman padded about the floor, he a had a length of paper sticking to one paw, Edwin eyed it and then took The Scotsman by surprise, lifting the paw to remove it. Edwin smiled at what was now a beautiful curve of paper and moved back to his desk. The Scotsman, somewhat disgruntled at the surprise attack, settled himself in his cardboard box.

The paper curled easily about his fingers. He pictured musical notes, imagined them positioned along a staff... a long strip of paper... or... a shorter piece... A particular musical phrase, *yes*... perhaps for the violin? – You see it on the page, notes dancing on a staff. You pluck it from the page... and curl it around your finger... looping round and up! Now freeze the image, enlarge, create a net... fill in the net making it solid. – Just a curl, a sail of paper, music rising up....

We will make it using concrete, maybe translucent... but also glass... yes, a musical phrase. – And the notes themselves informing other elements. – *The violin!* Yes! The music itself must be for the violin!

It might occur to those who knew Edwin well that his choice of music may have had less to do with Charles and Gaia Ore than it did with a very particular woman from Edwin's own past. For didn't he used to know someone who could play the violin rather well, and wasn't that someone a long lost love named Lizzie? Lizzie, who had once broken his heart?

Edwin would never allow himself to acknowledge this connection consciously, but he wondered at moments why he had been so certain that the music simply had to have been for the violin. No matter, he thought. His *Frozen Music* was taking shape, and all this spontaneity only added to his excitement. A house of music, filled with light!

A curl of paper, a curve of paper... this was enough, a place from which to begin. And now he must consider the dweller's daily life... the acoustics of the building – this would be most important, he might design a complete sound system... but was there time? Music and light. What better way to heal a grieving heart.

Edwin would have his design team work around the clock on this project. It was 6am, they began to arrive. The computer animation for this would be nothing short of state of the art, but Edwin insisted the team slow down the speed of these visuals, he would not have them as ridiculously fast paced as they'd been apt to run things of late. The most recent fly-throughs he'd seen literally sent his head spinning. If high speed flight through a design of several floors didn't set off a fit or at very least a migraine, nothing would! His animators were among the best, that he knew, but Lordy, slow it down! The team regularly teased the architect about not keeping up with technology. He hastened to point out that they were not employed in the world of computer games, faced by sharp shooters round every corner, or alien-zombies shooting up through false floors, and he tersely reminded them how architectural greenhorns were ten-a-penny to replace. They shut up, and designed as instructed. What's more, Edwin was right, and when push came to shove their alien-zombie heads knew it.

Chapter Twenty-six

Seduction

Today Alessandro is out at his office. Left alone, Gaia bathes, then wanders about his enchanting home. She settles lazily in the sunshine. The windows overlooking the gardens let in a pale warm heat. Drops of sunshine shimmer in the air.

She runs over Selené's last letters to Charles. The final three. Lying naked now, and contented, she reads them over and over, recasting the voice as her own, and Alessandro, as the recipient.

From Letter 1

Selené to Charles

I think you star architects wait far too long before designing the 'dream home', why wait?

I can sense that my teasing might make you mad, still – you must allow a girl her fun. I'd certainly never keep your attention if I did but only adore you, and adore you, I do....

From Letter 2

Selené to Charles

...it is a woman's want to inspire the flame of man from time to time.

...some of us have the good sense to keep you men at a wise and comfortable distance appropriate to our same requirements of say, the changes in season.

From Letter 3

Selené to Charles

I so love to tease, but that's always the way, and passions always peak in the wake of, and fear of losing them. Oh I am too cruel again. Forgive me, but the grass has been freshly cut, and I am of a mind to take... a lover.

That luscious minted air, arouses me more than the scent of any man, but then my affinity has always been with nature....

Gaia grew passionate, laughing, wild. Selené, she must write to her.

Letter: Lover
Gaia to Selené

Dear Selené,

Oh, what shall I tell you? And how? I must remain calm and composed, but it's not possible, I feel so blissfully drunk, with life!

If I am to write anything sensible at all, I must keep my thoughts ordered. Firstly, I have decided to stay on here, I don't know for how long, at least until the competition is through, and this relates to another important point… Alessandro, *the Italian*, has suggested that the competitors gather here in Italy to present their work, and I am going to accept, though I am beginning to worry about the press and our privacy. I must protect the competitors, for this was never intended as a news story and I can see how easily it might become one. But perhaps we can create a diversion, a press release with false locations… something of that order. So much to consider! But I know that Alessandro will help me all he can. And I am becoming so excited by it all, Selené. – The finale! It is no time away at all now, and it would make me so happy if you would also come. *I know, I know, but please!*

I would so love to meet you!

Secondly, I have now had plenty of time to consider what I might do with the *Construct*. I have filled so many notebooks with ideas and possibilities while I've been here, and I've walked so many miles… my mind has finally begun to find some clarity. And so, it occurs to me that many of the *units* would make perfect music rooms, some might even be soundproofed and adapted to be used as studio space for recording. I have decided to make the building over to my mailman, and now friend, Tom Bradshaw. I think Charles would also approve and so it seems fitting. I will make over a sum of money to him also, for running costs and so forth, a kind of sponsorship, so to speak.

And thirdly, Italy is proving a wonderful lift to my spirit, and Alessandro also. I would not have believed it possible, but find myself bathed in desire.

What has happened to me? I lay now, reading over the lines of your letters, planning to play them out as I venture now to seduce this man. Is it very wicked of me to use them so?

My deepest affection

Gaia

Letter: Architect

Selené to Gaia

My dear sweet Gaia,

Your words, as always, are dear to me. It seems that Italy suits you rather well, rejoice! The Italian suits you also! Make love with him! It seems there is precious little that I can instruct or advise upon, and therefore, I rejoice!

But darling Gaia, do not seduce with the words of another, it is not honest, it is not true. You must find words that are your own. You must take the courage to be architect of your own life.

I will not come to Italy.

My love to you now, and always

Selené

Chapter Twenty-seven
Desire

Alessandro was familiar with the English phrase, *bloody awful,* and now, whilst sneaking an intimate peek at Gaia's *rock-climbing-carcasses* – with the aim of discovering her shoe size – he felt he finally had an appropriate context in which to use it. Soft, worn-in leather, so worn-in that it stank, bloody awful!

Small feet, delicate. Time for a surprise gift! Salvatore Ferragamo!

Alessandro was in his element, Gaia was clearly comfortable in his home, she seemed to have an affinity with Italy, and with him? Rapport *and…* he pinched himself, afraid of how much he hoped for, of how deeply desirous he had grown. – Shoes! He must remain focused, but quite inexplicably, it was now with trepidation that he ventured to choose this special secret gift.

So, *what colour, what design, material, and texture?* There was so much to consider. Gaia Ore. Beautiful, ethereal. She concealed, challenged. She was, at times, impossible to impress; at others, happy to find amazement in things too ordinary to contemplate. Gaia. Ah, it was tricky, finding the right shoe for Gaia, very tricky. Alessandro forced a smile, to find some humour and lighten the spirit, but the shoes displayed before him in the shop just now only perplexed. He felt too hot, then shivered. What was wrong? What was happening? *Gaia, what do you do to me?*

All these long weeks, his desire for her was so intense, and the more intense, the less he felt able to seduce. – Shoes… black. Should they be black? Those tiny feet. Black? He ran his fingers over the surface of the shoes, cold patent, soft suede, warm leather, stiff. What's wrong? The shoes, such shoes, such heavenly shoes, but no, *no more!* He had to get out. A man realising he had unwittingly mastered nothing more than his own romantic cliché.

Gaia, what power do you wield that I am become a man quite lost? Suddenly I am made uneasy, agitated, I fear your rejection, your leaving, somehow even your staying, and I can share nothing of this with you. What happens? What happens if you reject my affections? It would be natural, for you are a woman in mourning, a woman of whom I have made a dear friend, a woman who is wanting of nothing more. If you leave, it will be because you must, because you must continue your life, make a home of your new house. If you stay, I fear, just fear, and I am tormented now by this – I will disappoint you, fail you, even make you sad, for I have not the confidence that I could cheer you, as I once so wished I might. *Gaia, Gaia*. No, I must compose myself, I must maintain some distance, and not make more confusion. I would make you a gift of all the great shoes of the world, *of anything, of everything*, but somehow it's not right. I am losing my head! Losing my way. No shoes, no gifts, nothing!

Friendship, yes… the competition will end, you will leave, and I, I will carry on. Of course, that is all natural. All as it should be. As it will be.

Nervously, he walked the streets to clear his mind, going back to his office to drown in work awhile. There would soon be visitors, the other competitors, and there was much to prepare. Hotel rooms to book, cars to be arranged, caterers. At least, he determined, playing host to the guests was something he would make a definite success of. It would be wonderful to see Ralph. As always, it had been too long since he'd seen his good friend, and how marvellous to meet with the others, and this… this was to be Gaia's moment, he should keep that in mind. Yes, he must concentrate on his original intention, to help in her recovery, to lighten her mood, to restore to her some cheer – this extended vacation would hopefully achieve that in some measure. He should not have hoped for more. She looked very well in Italy, he should feel proud, glad! And that, that was enough. The competition… it was a marvellous architectural adventure; soon Gaia would choose her favourite design and eventually she would be able to settle again, and enjoy her new home.

He was angry with himself, feeling arrogant and foolish for all his great ambitions to seduce, his great desire that she might love him, and his secret hope that she might stay.

Chapter Twenty-eight
The Architectural Finale

Gaia had been very astute about the press, rumours had indeed begun to spread, and a small ripple was gradually moving outwards gathering driftwood on the way; if she did not act swiftly and with cunning there would soon be a media deluge. Fortunately Alessandro was only too pleased to assist, and fresh rumours were quickly circulated to counter stories of their true whereabouts, the existence of a very private competition and the names of the competitors. Ernest Wrightsin was pretty certain that the finale would be held in Romania, a clever choice, completely unpretentious, a location few would think of. Others speculated that it would be in New Zealand, but where in New Zealand? No one was quite sure. Maybe it would be in Texas. Some said Ireland. Despite the work involved in setting these fanciful stories running, it did pay off. The misinformation worked well for the most part and was the cause of much amusement to the architect guests soon to arrive in Italy.

The guests very quickly and obligingly settled themselves in, few special dietary requests and no complaints, for all that ego they would not play the prima donna here. Gaia ran through the itinerary for the day of the finale itself. If they wouldn't mind, she would like the proceedings to begin with a few words each from Edwin and Alessandro – Edwin as the most senior in age, Alessandro as the host. She had decided to save her own words until after the architectural works had been shown. It seemed a wise move, allowing her to retain a small amount of distance from the competitors, that she might apply a degree of critical objectivity, and focus her attention on the designs and presentations without the encumbrance and distraction of first delivering a speech.

There had been so much to consider, and *now*, now they were here! Would that they had enjoyed the challenge, would that they enjoyed their stay in Italy, and the finale itself. She had asked so much of them... and was it *too* much?

The Day Had Come…

Before embarking on his opening speech, Edwin Ray first took Gaia to one side, "May I just say Mrs Ore, that I think this is a tremendous and most fitting way to celebrate the memory of Charles, *Grand Architect,* and indeed your very dear husband." Gaia smiled enigmatically before moving away to the comfort of champagne.

It was a select gathering, four world class architects, the ghost of another, the good will of Selené, and Gaia herself. She looked into her glass as Edwin Ray began his speech. At first it seemed it was entirely in remembrance and celebration of *The Great, Charles Ore*. Edwin, soon in full flow. – But Gaia did not hear his ebullient memento mori, but rather her own internal words of anger as they streamed through her mind now, completely unbidden.

The competition was to design a home for me! Charles, lest you not forget, is dead. My husband was known to contenders, critics and admirers alike as *The Architect of the Age*, and as such, to each of you, he holds the place of hero, of accomplice or enemy, but that doesn't matter anymore, he's dead! And so too *The Age* in which, and for which, he designed. I gave you each the most open remit, now let us see what you have done!

She felt a shudder as her thoughts jolted back to the present moment. Her mind raced, but she must stay calm; she took her seat and listened now to Edwin Ray.

"Politicians, despite understanding so little, always attempt to avoid taking part in the *real* adventure of architecture…."

Ralph Coover interrupted, "Yeah, *Risky,* they call it!" A considered smile crossed the room.

Edwin picked up again, "Too much caution… that's the usual run of things. Of course I understand some elements of this, but we must avoid the indescribably banal that previous generations have given in to… the hyper-traditional over-build, the repetition! Things we are all too familiar with. – Anyway, each of us… in our own way… seems to have carved himself from the cloth of the rebel architect, and if I do not make myself gauche in saying so, I think Mrs Ore has truly gathered here the *ultimate* rebel set. – Speaking for myself at least, I have to say that this competition and the process I have engaged in has been a wonderful re-acquaintance with the basics, the fundamentals, with the absolute joy and playfulness of architecture, and my approach has largely been 'back to basics'. One I have most thoroughly enjoyed."

Coover raised his hands and applauded. He had thought to add a "Here, here!" but was cautious of sounding mocking; this was a competition alright, but he found himself incredibly moved by the whole encounter. Their coming together quite like this was something such great adversaries would seldom do, and so it had required the widow of a former adversary, and a competition the likes of which they had never seen. And Edwin was right, this had been a real grassroots experience; sitting alone with pencils, paints, and charcoal, tearing up paper, crafting little models. Thrusting their hands deep into the soil again.

A modest little house, this was the kind of project Coover felt he had largely missed out on, it was what his soul was missing of late, and dirty fingernails had never felt so good. He looked over his calloused hands in deep admiration. They didn't pull in the ladies, they did do a mean old sketch.

Edwin was fizzing in champagne by now, the bubbles seeming to pop from an emboldened brow. He scratched his beard, "There are times when both my methods and my designs have been seen to cause provocation, but really, this is what is required – or we will all fall into a deep complacent slumber – architects, dwellers, all." He laid down his glass.

Edwin had finished speaking, and after Alessandro's speech it would be time for the architects to present their designs. Gaia felt distant again, the initial gentle silence that followed Edwin's closing words now slipping away, awkwardness filtering through.

Her thoughts grew cynical as bereavement reared, and she grew afraid. What might they have done? How had they attempted this task? Her head, suddenly terrorised by scenes of how aggressively Charles would have met with such a challenge. Sleep-working, frantic sketching, irascible and bullying, ego-fired. Competing, always competing, with his peers, and certainly with all who had gone before him. Might these architects have done the same? Had they now designed to compete with the dead, with their memory of Charles? Or perhaps, they had designed in adoration... might they have designed an altar to him? *Is that what I have asked for?* An architectural collage to compete with his own works? Should I want even to lie in such a thing, a crude mutation of his own designs, in materials he would favour? Or do I even want to be reminded of such things? Will they have remembered that this was to be... a house of my own?

Her cheeks coloured with the fear that any of them might read her thoughts. Thoughts too emotional, irrational and all unkind. The wrong-thinking went before her. She must gather herself, tear herself from memories and pains. That was done with, that was past. The present time, and the people here gathered, deserved a careful appreciation of all that had actually been designed, in tenderness, in detail and with passion.

Edwin now passed the baton to Alessandro, "Thank you, Mr Ray, and so... I hope I am not too bold in speaking on behalf of all of us like this, but I think that I may be right in saying that this has been a wonderful project and challenge. Most importantly, I feel that this generous and open remit has been a way of keeping things fresh... and soft – something Mr Ray has also touched upon – indulging again those youthful and vigorous thought processes where we could permit the primacy of imagination and creativity with very little restraint. There are few clients who would ever have allowed our minds, talents and skill such freedoms. For my part, I have not enjoyed architecture so much since I was a small boy!" The room filled with warmth and laughter. "I have been able to revisit some methods of working that over time I may have lost. Working only on large scale projects, moving too much to the dictates of too powerful clients, we... or I, can feel constrained, impeded, frustrated... and deep inside is still the desire and ambition to run free, to take a small idea, to keep the mind and fingers soft, to take the seedling, find that perfect spot, plant and let it grow, to take the ideas, the imagination, keep them malleable... make something new, appropriate, thoughtful. Something for someone else but clearly with your own prints embedded there. Something new emerges, ideas made manifest. With the big projects, we are aware and can enjoy the team dynamic, but so many demands press in on us, the client always hovering in the wings somehow. Anyway, as

Coover knows more than any other here, I will talk and talk and talk if permitted to," Coover smiled, he loved the sound of his name in Zandro's tones, "but I wanted to take a moment to reflect, for during this project I have certainly experienced some joyous moments of breakthrough. So, thank you, Mrs Ore... Gaia."

"Indeed, indeed!" called Edwin Ray, and sounds of approval filled the room.

Edwin Ray now gently whispered into Gaia's ear, "Mrs Ore, what do you think? Are you ready now... might we begin to present the designs?"

"The designs. Yes, of course," she was happy, "Shall we take a look?"

They moved to the adjoining room.

It took a number of hours to work through all the presentations. Models, animations, explanations... Gaia drifted in reflection as their words glided through their magnificent designs.

Ralph Coover's – Globe
Alessandro Cannizzaro's – Eyrie
Carlos Santillana's – Pebble
Edwin Ray's – Frozen Music

The intellect! The potency! The spontaneity! And brilliance! And what tears came now. Powerful, appreciative, heartfelt.

At the close of the presentations the assembled group retired for the day, each free to set out and explore their host's local environs, or to seize some rare and precious time alone. They might relax awhile and sleep away the journeying or muse upon the day's events. They would meet again at dusk.

Evening came. Gaia would speak. A winner would be chosen. A most wonderful dinner would be shared.

It was Gaia's moment. Carlos stood calmly, a pebble in his pocket; Coover sat astride a broad wooden bench, quietly confident, the promise of an announcement, and then of good food, seemed like a result! Edwin appeared cheerful and animated, glass of red in hand; and Alessandro, Alessandro feigned a quiet confidence, but his heart was a flutter. Was this going how she wanted? Was the event a success? And had he made the other competitors comfortable enough? Was the hotel to their liking? But mostly his thoughts settled on Gaia. – Had she found a design that she liked? Just four competitors! They might all have failed her... And then finally... finally... she spoke, "I could hardly have hoped that any of you would even consider, let alone accept my wild proposition, and yet... you did. You did, and each of you has shown such great sincerity, thoughtfulness, and energy. And you have worked quite as I had hoped, though dared not dream, with equal care and consideration of both the inside space and the outside. You have thought about how a person might dwell in the place that you have made. And you have also thought how I would most feel comfortable.

"As different as your designs are one from another, and your methods also I suspect, I chose you each for the single attribute I most admire in an architect... rigour. For you each apply rigour in all things, at all stages.

"Outside is in, inside is out... you are concerned about mood, and light, and most importantly to me... you take care of the culture of the dweller. These are the ingredients of great work... and with such intense rigour applied... well, that's quite an equation." A ripple of warmth circled the room.

Gaia looked the models over again, "I gave you almost no time at all to produce these works... and look!" Her heart was filled; the architects' also. "Just look at this great harvest!"

Coover bowed his head, afraid of blushes. Edwin smiled broadly, and puffed out his chest, would The Scotsman were here, a tail would certainly be wagging. Carlos had pulled himself up almost on tiptoes, the sunshine of praise causing him to blossom. And Alessandro... blushed from head to toe.

"And why do I so adore architecture?" She paused a moment, warm emotion rising, she must not lose the last few words, "That's an easy one to answer. It is simply the discipline which encapsulates all others. The profession and art I most admire.

"From all of you, I have learned a very great deal. You work, each of you, with tremendous passion… and zeal. I think I can say that I love that in each of you."

– *So how would she choose?*
– *And who would she choose?*

"Each one of you, in your own distinct way, has managed to design… to design a home, a perfect home, for me.

"I conclude," she breathed, "that this… will necessitate the construction… of all four designs. Four builds! Let us make four homes. I love them all, and so, let's build each one! Such is my own, and your, deep love for architectural works, I truly think it will take all four to satisfy such thirst! –I clearly cannot live in all four, extravagance on that scale would not sit easy with me, but we will find good use for each of them. For certain we will. – And I will not divide them in order of merit. Look at them, it would be impossible. – And… if he is agreeable, I will put my trust in Alessandro… to find the perfect site for each."

Chapter Twenty-nine
Home

Letter: In Words of my Own
Gaia to Alessandro

My dear Alessandro,
As you read this letter, I lie awaiting you in the adjoining room.
Do not move, do not venture in.
Be still, read me, alone, in the quiet, and when the reading is over,
When the ink has run its course, then come.
Here, near to you, I sense a kinship I have never known, and will never know
again.
Here, as I have watched you, I feel desire such that I have never known,
And will never want to know again, for it is desire entwined with pain.
If the desire is met, if it is fulfilled, perhaps it will nourish – until then,
I will hurt with the deepest physical pain, emotional... physical, the same now.
Images run through my head, sensual, crazed.
Tears of passion flow from cheek to breast, and you?
Undress my sweet.
Would that I could feel that intense heart push through your flesh
And bleed close to mine
Just flesh
I do not need a house
I do not need a home
Not glass, nor stone, but a house, a home, of flesh
I need a house
I need a home
Of flesh, of the senses, and spontaneous design
Your hands, my skin

Your skin, my warmth
Wrapped, swathed, in nakedness
Just skin
Alessandro, I am, with you, most passionately, in love
I do not need a house
I do not need a home
But that of your sweet skin next mine

Gaia

Acknowledgments

Particular thanks go to: Joerg Rainer Noennig, Christopher Knabe, Mickaël Postel, Catherine Mauduit, Greta Dowling Flaherty, and June Zhao.

Huge thanks go out to all the friends and family who have supported me along the way; and a special thank you to all at Alcemi, especially Gwen Davies; and to my agent, Melissa Pimentel at Curtis Brown.

I would like to thank the Welsh Books Council for their continued support.

I am grateful both to the RIBA and the V&A for their public lecture series; and to the RIBA for answering a writer's naive questions. I am also grateful to the architects who have helped with technical detail, and to others for inspiration. I am sure to have taken liberties with what might truly work in the real world, and so, whilst inspired and guided by experts I have most blissfully indulged the imagination to create the buildings of a fictional one.

As for my own notebooks on architecture (the starting point for this novel), they began their adventure quite without purpose when I was living in Japan (mostly as a series of small sketches and observations). I kept up the notebooks as I travelled back through Europe and home to the UK. After this, they came along with me to China, and after some time there, back again to the UK, gently zigzagging their way across the map. Glad I started them. Glad I kept them.

The Gallery

An artist's impression
of the houses featured in the novel

by
Hiroki Godengi

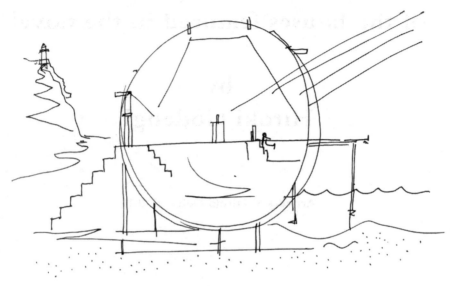

Globe   Hiroki Golovff

'Frozen Music' Hiroshi Sadoshima

Pebble

Hinker Godesff

Eyrie

Hiroki Sodenji

www.alcemi.eu

Talybont Ceredigion Cymru SY24 5HE
e-mail gwen@ylolfa.com
phone (01970) 832 304
fax (01970) 832 782

ALCEMI A